Whose
They

An American Farce

by Michael Parker

A SAMUEL FRENCH ACTING EDITION

FOUNDED 1830

SAMUELFRENCH.COM

ISBN   978-0-573-62966-2   Printed in U.S.A.   #252

MUSIC USE NOTE

IMPORTANT BILLING AND CREDIT REQUIREMENTS

Whose Wives Are They Anyway?

AN AMERICAN FARCE

by

MICHAEL PARKER

was first produced at the Delray Beach Playhouse,
Delray Beach, Florida
on October 1st, 1998

The Cast

JOHN BAKER	Michael DeGrotta
DAVID McGACHEN	Marc Streeter
TINA	Ann Patrice Gomersall
MRS. CARLSON	Jodie Dixon
WILSON	Jack Gordon
D.L. HUTCHISON	Charlotte Sherman
KARLY McGACHEN	Nedria DeGrotta
LAURA BAKER	Marcie Hall

Directed by Randolph Del Lago
Designed by Ann Cadaret

Original title:
WHOSE WIFE IS IT ANYWAY?

CHARACTERS

JOHN BAKER *(age 35-40)*: A vice president of The Ashley Maureen Cosmetics Corporation, he is a successful business executive, who, because of his kind and gentle nature, allows himself to be manipulated into compromising situations by the more dominant personality of David. Alternating between the roles of himself and David's "wife," he is caught up in a whirlwind of events beyond his control, but nevertheless manages to show great strength of character and personality. *(Hardworking, honest, straightforward and full of initiative.)*

DAVID McGACHEN *(age 45-50)*: A distinguished looking man, he has risen to become a vice president of The Ashley Maureen Cosmetics Corporation more by guile and cunning than ability and hard work. Relentless in his efforts to impress his new boss, he attempts to manipulate all those around him. Even when his plan to create two alternative wives begins to unravel, he never gives up scheming and plotting, and always seems to come up with "one more idea." *(Clever and cunning, a relentless schemer.)*

TINA *(age 20-30)*: The young, pretty country club receptionist. She is good at her job, impressing the guests with her smile and personality. Once she has been persuaded to impersonate John's wife, she embraces the role wholeheartedly. After a little too much champagne, she seems to have difficulty keeping all her clothes on, and ends up at the heart of many of the visual comic sequences. *(Bright, sexy, a bubbling personality.)*

MRS. CARLSON *(age 45-55)*: The club manager. A straight-laced, severe woman who, in a few years will no doubt become a typical "old battleaxe." At this stage in her life she prefers to take the moral high ground, and does not hesitate to preach the evils of sex and adultery. She sees herself as guardian of morality for the country club, and makes sure all her guests know it. *(Dominant, bossy, efficient, yet rather likeable.)*

WILSON *(age 60+)*: The club handyman. He is the complete and total hypochondriac. You name it, he suffers from it! An endearing and comic character, he lights up the stage at his every entrance with his chronic complaints. Never far from most of the comic sequences, he is a pivotal character who observes all the madcap happenings going on around him. *(Likeable, funny, with a great sense of humor.)*

D.L. HUTCHISON *(age 45-50)*: The new president of The Ashley Maureen Cosmetics Corporation. She is bright, smart and self-assured, with a "take charge" nature. She is the "straight man" of the plot, for whose benefit the duplicate wives have been produced. She is a somewhat overbearing character, serious in nature, who, at all times, is all business. She is finally revealed as a duplicitous hypocrite in the surprise ending. *(Smart, attractive, efficient and personable.)*

KARLY McGACHEN *(age 40ish)*: She is quite a strong character who reacts in a positive and forceful way to the apparent infidelity of her husband David. Determined to make him jealous, she is party to several hilarious scenes as she makes a play for the reluctant Wilson. *(Determined and calculating, yet with a tender side.)*

LAURA BAKER *(age 30-40)*: A pretty little thing who is somewhat dominated by the stronger character of Karly, she is a simple soul who just wants to love and be loved by her husband John. She never quite understands what is going on around her. She cries at the drop of a hat, and spends much of her time on stage in tears. *(Tender, loving, naive.)*

SETTING

The action of the play takes place in the reception area,
and rooms 11 and 13, of The Oakfield Golf and Country Club,
somewhere in New England.

TIME: The Present

ACT I:
Early Friday evening in August

ACT II:
The action is continuous

ACT I

*(The curtain rises on an empty set. It is the reception area, hallway
and guest rooms 11 and 13 of The Oakfield Golf and Country
Club.*

*The entranceway, D.R., leads to the bar, dining room and front en-
trance to the club. R. is the reception area, with a small counter,
which has a call bell and a telephone on it, behind which is a
double-hinged door to the office. U.R.C. are two or three steps to
a landing with a railing each side of them. In the center of the U.S.
wall on the landing is the door to room 8. The landing continues
off R. to other rooms and the terrace, and off L. to rooms 11, 13
and the pro-shop.*

*The L. 60-65% of the stage consists of rooms 11 and 13 which are
built up to the same level as the landing. The walls are all cut
out, with the exception of the U.S. walls and the connecting
pocket door between the two rooms, which is closed. Each room
has a double bed and a bedside table with a reading lamp and
telephone on it. The tables are R. of the bed in room 11 and L. of
the bed in room 13. Room 11, to the R. of room 13, has a bathroom U.R. of the bed. Room 13 has a bathroom D.L. of the bed.
These two rooms are of equal size and identical in decor.*

*D.R.C. in the reception area is a small couch with an afghan neatly
folded over it. To its L. is a low backed easy chair. Between them
is a small side table with a telephone and a newspaper on it.*

*After a few moments, JOHN BAKER and DAVID McGACHEN enter
from the front entrance. JOHN, age about 40, is a fairly quiet,
mild mannered man, overshadowed a little, as we shall see, by
the more dominant personality of DAVID, but nevertheless a successful executive, who knows what he wants in life. He is the vice*

*president in charge of marketing for The Ashley Maureen Cos-
metics Corporation. DAVID, perhaps 45-50, is a tall, distinguished looking man, who has risen to become the vice president
in charge of franchise operations for the Ashley Maureen Corporation, more by guile and cunning than ability or hard work.
Both are dressed casually, ready for the golf course, and carry small
suitcases, which they put down by the counter.)*

DAVID. *(Looking around as he enters.)* Not a bad little place,
not bad at all. *(He rings the call bell.)* We'll get checked in and we'll
just have time for nine holes before dinner.

JOHN. Do you think we've got time? It's nearly five o'clock.

DAVID. You betcha. It doesn't get dark till about 8.

JOHN. Well, I guess we could then.

DAVID. We've got to make the most of the weekend. Your idea
to send our wives to New York, so they could go shopping for the
whole weekend was brilliant. *(He rings the call bell again.)* Come on
Come on.

JOHN. It might just be the most expensive idea I've ever had
Have you any idea how much damage those two can do on Fifth Avenue?

*(Enter TINA from the office. She is young and very pretty. Age 20-30
she is bright and personable, well suited to her job as the receptionist. She is wearing a dark fitted skirt, a brightly colored long
sleeve silk blouse, hose and high heels.)*

TINA. I'm sorry if I kept you waiting, but the phone system in the
entire building is in the process of being rewired. This one *(She indicates the counter phone.)* doesn't seem to work at all, so I had to take
a call in the office.

JOHN. Oh that's alright, we've only been here a minute.

TINA. You must be the two guys from the Ashley Maureen Cosmetics Company I spoke to this morning.

DAVID. That's right, I'm David McGachen, and this is John
Baker.

TINA. Hi! I'm Tina. Could you fill these in please. *(She puts two forms on the counter as the phone on the side table rings.)* Good grief, that can't ring, it's not an outside line. *(She crosses L. to pick up the phone as JOHN and DAVID fill in the forms.)* Hello, what? No I can not put twenty dollars on Little Green Man in the 4:30 at Belmont. This is The Oakfield Golf and Country Club. That's alright. Goodbye. *(She hangs up and returns behind the counter.)* The worst part is the phone company people all left at four o'clock, and you know we won't get anything done now till Monday morning. *(They hand her the forms.)* Two singles for two nights, right?

JOHN. Right.

TINA. I always use it you know.

JOHN. Use what?

TINA. Ashley Maureen make-up.

JOHN. Oh good. I'm sure I've got some samples in the car. I'll get you some later.

TINA. Ooh thank you. What do you guys do for the company?

JOHN. Well, I'm the vice president in charge of marketing, and David here is the vice president for franchise operations.

TINA. You here on business or pleasure?

DAVID. Strictly pleasure. We're here to play golf till we drop. It'll probably be the last chance we get for quite a while.

TINA. Oh?

JOHN. You might have read it in the paper, but Ashley Maureen has just been taken over by the Stratford Corporation. The new president starts on Monday, so I don't think we'll be taking another long weekend for a while.

TINA. Well, I bet you have a terrific weekend. I've put you in rooms 11 and 13, and the pro shop is just past room 13 at the end of the hallway.

JOHN. Oh, we should bring the golf bags in here then?

TINA. Yes, I'll get someone to carry them for you.

(Enter MRS. CARLSON from U.R. She is a rather severe looking woman, somewhat dour and taciturn, who does not seem to enjoy life very much and appears to resent people who do. Age perhaps 50, she is very conservative in dress, with little or no make-up and her hair up in a bun or French roll.)

MRS. C. *(Comes D.)* Good afternoon gentlemen. You must be the people from The Ashley Maureen Corporation. I'm Mrs. Carlson. I'm the manager of the club.

DAVID. *(Shakes hands.)* I'm David McGachen, how do you do? And this is John Baker.

JOHN. *(Shakes hands.)* I'm pleased to meet you.

MRS. C. How do you do? Now is there anything I can do for you?

DAVID. Thank you, but this young lady is taking very good care of us.

TINA. Have you seen Wilson?

MRS. C. I just left him. He's sweeping leaves out on the terrace.

TINA. I need him to carry some bags. Can you hold the fort for a minute?

MRS. C. Of course.

TINA. Won't be a minute.

(Exits U.R. The counter phone rings.)

MRS. C. *(Picks up the phone.)* Oakfield Golf and Country Club. You want me to what? A "C" note on the nose of a little green man? Why in heaven's name would you want me to put anything on the nose of a little green man? Because who scratched? Listen young man, I don't know who you are, or what you want, but I am not going to enter into any discussion about who is scratching what. *(She hangs up.)* I really must apologize gentlemen. I take great pride in the fact that I manage a club that is usually the very model of propriety and decorum. I'm afraid these mixed up phone calls are just driving us all crazy.

(She busies herself with papers behind the desk.)

DAVID. I wonder what he'll be like?

JOHN. Who?

DAVID. The new president of the company, D.L. Hutchison.

JOHN. I don't know, but I've heard the Stratford Corporation run a really tight ship.

DAVID. Oh?

JOHN. I've heard they get all involved in your private life, and if you don't do things their way, you're out.

DAVID. Oh boy! We're going to have to watch it. You know that old saying, "a new broom sweeps clean."

Enter TINA from the U.R. landing. She is followed by WILSON. He is dressed in tan pants and a colored golf shirt with the club logo embroidered on it. Age perhaps 60, he is a crotchety old geezer who wouldn't be happy if he had nothing to complain about, and appears to be resentful of everything and everyone.)

TINA. *(Coming D. from the landing.)* Here you are gentlemen. This is Wilson. He'll help you with the bags.

WILSON. Golf bags are they?

JOHN. Yes, of course.

WILSON. I've got a bad back you know.

JOHN. Oh dear, perhaps I should help you then.

MRS. C. Wilson! Don't take any notice of him, he's perfectly fit.

JOHN. Well there's two golf bags, so why don't I help him anyway. Come on Wilson.

He exits to the front entrance.)

WILSON. *(Following him.)* That's very kind of you sir, if it wasn't for this hernia of mine I'd be able to—

TINA. *(Laughing.)* You'll get used to Wilson, everybody does. *The phone in the office rings.)* I'll get it.

Exits to office.
The door to room 8 opens and D.L. HUTCHISON comes down the steps. She is a handsome woman, age 45-50, very smartly dressed in a pastel colored two piece suit, high heels and conservative accessories. She is what you might expect of the C.E.O. of a multimillion dollar corporation, smart, intelligent, bright and self-assured.)

MRS. C. *(Hands DAVID a key.)* Here you are Mr. McGachen. I

see Tina's put you in room 13, up the steps and second on your right.

DAVID. Thank you.

(MRS. C. exits to the office.)

D.L. *(Comes D.)* Excuse me, Mr. McGachen?

DAVID. Yes.

D.L. Mr. David McGachen?

DAVID. Yes.

D.L. Do you by any chance happen to work for the Ashley Maureen Corporation?

DAVID. Yes, as a matter of fact, I do.

D.L. You have a rather uncommon name, so I thought it must be you. Allow me to introduce myself. I'm D.L. Hutchison, from The Stratford Corporation, and your new president at Ashley Maureen.

DAVID. *(Shakes hands.)* How do you do? *(Just a little flustered.)* How did you know who I am?

D.L. *(Crosses L. to sit in the chair, and gestures to David that he should sit on the couch.)* Oh, I've been studying the personnel files of all the executives. I like to know as much as possible about the people who work for me.

DAVID. *(Sits.)* I see.

D.L. Our corporate policy is to play an active role in the off-duty lives of our employees. We believe a happy executive is a productive executive.

DAVID. Quite right D.L.

D.L. So, you here for the weekend?

DAVID. Yes we're just checking in.

D.L. Good, I'm here for the weekend too. I'm in room 8. You know this is a wonderful coincidence, we must make the most of the opportunity.

DAVID. We must?

D.L. Yes, of course. I have the chance to meet you and your wife and get to know you both a little, before we all get down to work on Monday.

DAVID. My wife?

D.L. Of course. She is here with you.isn't she?

DAVID. Well actually she's gone shopping—

D.L. Excellent. I'll meet her when she gets back here then. You know, confidentially, just between the two of us, if there's one thing I simply can't tolerate, it's men who go off to play golf on the weekend without their wives. No one like that will ever work for me. I want my executives to be very involved with their families.

DAVID. You do?

D.L. Yes indeed. *(Stands.)* I'll look forward to meeting your wife. Shall we say cocktails before dinner? Let's meet here about six then.

DAVID. *(Stands.)* Well actually—

D.L. Good, that's settled then. I'll see you later.

(Exits up the steps and into room 8. Enter JOHN and WILSON from the front entrance, each carrying a large golf bag.)

WILSON. It puts a strain on your intestines you know, carrying loads like this.

DAVID. John, we're in trouble.

JOHN. What?

DAVID. Quick let's get into our rooms.

JOHN. I haven't even got a key yet. *(DAVID is pounding the call bell.)* What in heaven's name is going on?

(TINA enters from the office.)

DAVID. Have you got Mr. Baker's key?

TINA. Right here sir, number eleven.

(She hands him a key.)

DAVID. *(Picks up both cases.)* Good, hurry.

(He leads the way up the steps, then L. on the landing, followed by JOHN and WILSON carrying the golf bags.)

WILSON. I knew a guy once, got a ruptured spleen from carrying golf bags.

TINA. Wilson, could I see you in the office when you've finished please?

(Exits to office.)

WILSON. *(Now at the top of the stairs.)* I'd sprint right down, miss, but my shin splints are giving me all sorts of problems today.

(Exits L. on the landing.)

JOHN. *(Opening the door of room 11 and talking to DAVID over his shoulder.)* Just calm down, let's at least get into our rooms. Boy this is small. *(He walks around the bed and opens the bathroom door.)* That's better, there's a dressing room as well as a bathroom.

(He leaves the golf bag in the bathroom, comes back to the door, picks up his suitcase from outside the door and puts it on the bed. Meanwhile, DAVID has opened the door of room 13, and put his suitcase in the bathroom. WILSON has now stopped in the doorway of room 13 and taken the golf bag off his shoulder. DAVID then notices the connecting door, slides it open and goes into room 11.)

DAVID. Listen, John, we're in all sorts of trouble.

(WILSON reacts and leans forward to listen.)

JOHN. What are you talking about?
DAVID. I've just met D.L. Hutchison.
JOHN. He's here?
DAVID. Worse than that. She's here.
JOHN. She?
DAVID. She.
JOHN. So? *(WILSON is now leaning forward trying to listen and JOHN, looking past DAVID, sees him through the open connecting door.)* Ahem!

(He nods towards WILSON.)

DAVID. *(Realizes WILSON is still there and turns back into room 13. He reaches for the golf bag, but WILSON, who is not about to surrender the bag until he has received a tip, clutches it tightly and backs away. DAVID takes a couple of bills out of his pocket and hands them to WILSON.)* Thank you Wilson. That'll be all.

WILSON. Thank you sir.

DAVID. I'll take that.

(WILSON hands him the golf bag and closes the door of room 13. A second or two later we see him come D. and exit to the office. DAVID props the bag against the bed in room 13 and returns to room 11.)

JOHN. So, D.L.'s a woman. What's she like?

DAVID. She wants to meet our wives.

JOHN So, what's wrong with that?

DAVID. You don't understand. She's staying here at the club and wants to meet our wives for cocktails at 6 o'clock tonight.

JOHN. Well, didn't you tell her they're not here?

DAVID. No, thank goodness.

JOHN. What?

DAVID. Get this. She said any man who went off to play golf on the weekend without his wife would never work for her.

JOHN. Oh boy!

DAVID. Oh boy is right. What are we going to do? We're dead if we don't produce our wives.

JOHN. What do you mean "we"? She doesn't know I'm here does she?

DAVID. Come to think of it, I guess not.

JOHN. Right. That's it then. I'm headed out of here and right back home.

DAVID. You can't leave me in this mess. What am I going to do?

JOHN. You can start a whole new career as an olive stuffer for all I care. I'm outta here.

DAVID. Very funny! Now let me think. I've got to find a wife by six o'clock and we know the girls will never be home before midnight, and then it's an hour's drive to get here ...*(He trails off, deep in thought.)* wait a minute, wait a minute. I've got an idea.

JOHN. What?

DAVID. Do you remember that play you were in a couple of years ago?

JOHN. What play?

DAVID. You know, the one where you escaped by dressing as a woman.

JOHN. Sure but—oh no!

DAVID. Why not?

JOHN. Because we'd never get away with it.

DAVID. Of course we could. Everybody said how convincing you were.

JOHN. Yes, but I had clothes and a wig and make-up.

DAVID. There's a dress shop in the lobby and a beauty parlor with wigs in the window, and the one thing we're certainly not short of is make-up.

JOHN. David, this is stupid.

DAVID. You've got to help me. After all if it had been you D.L had seen, I would have helped you.

JOHN.   Would you really?

DAVID. Of course, what are friends for?

JOHN. Alright, I'll stay and help. I'm just not convinced this is the way to go.

DAVID. O.K. Do you have a better idea?

JOHN. Well, not really—

DAVID. Well then?

JOHN. O.K. I think you're crazy, but O.K.

DAVID. Alright. Let's get you to the dress shop and the beauty parlor.

JOHN. What am I going to tell them in the shop?

DAVID. Tell them you're going to a costume party or something. Let's see if the coast is clear.

(Leaving the connecting door open, they exit room 11, closing the door and go R. on the landing. Meanwhile WILSON has entered from the office, followed by TINA, who is carrying a phone.)

TINA. Let's try changing this phone please Wilson. Maybe this one works, I'll be right back.

(Hands him the phone.)

WILSON. Alright, but I don't think it'll do any good, it's the wiring and this junction box under the counter that's all screwed up.
TINA. Try it anyway. *(Exits to office.)*

(WILSON takes the phone off the counter and bends down behind it. He is out of sight as JOHN and DAVID come down the steps.)

DAVID. O.K. It looks like it's all clear. Go and get the clothes and remember, get back to the room as quick as you can.
JOHN. Are you sure you want me to dress up as a woman?

(They have come D.R. just below the counter.)

DAVID. Yes. I definitely want you to be my wife. *(WILSON's head slowly appears over the counter top, mouth open, eyes bulging.)* Now get going, and remember as far as anyone else is concerned we're both in room 13.

(JOHN exits to the front entrance. DAVID turns to go U.S. WILSON ducks out of sight. DAVID goes back into room 13, closing the door, picks up the golf bag and goes into the bathroom. WILSON stands up, his mouth wide open.)

WILSON. I don't believe it!

(Enter D.L. from room 8. She comes down.)

D.L. Ah Wilson, I wonder if you could do something for me please?
WILSON. Well, as long as it doesn't place a strain on my hernited disc, I'd be pleased to.
D.L. Is there a florist's in the club?

WILSON. I'm afraid not miss, but there's one just on the corner we always use.

D.L. Good. I wonder if you could run *(WILSON reacts.)* well, walk down and get a nice bouquet of roses for the couple in room 13?

WILSON. Couple?

D.L. Yes.

WILSON. Room 13?

D.L. Yes.

WILSON. Roses?

D.L. Yes, I always think roses are so romantic, don't you?

WILSON Romantic?

D.L. Yes, they've managed to get away together for the weekend and I thought flowers would be nice.

WILSON. You want to send flowers to the couple in room 13? And I thought I'd seen it all. I don't believe it.

(Enter MRS. CARLSON from the office.)

MRS. C. Everything alright Mrs. Hutchison?

D.L. Yes, thank you. If it's alright, I've just asked Wilson to run out and get me some flowers.

WILSON. I don't run anywhere miss. You see I've got these flat feet and—

MRS. C. Of course it's alright. That's what we're here for, aren' we Wilson?

WILSON. Did I ever tell you I once got a carbuncle on my foot? The doctor said it could have been caused by running. Very painful it was. Funny thing, I had it for years, and then one morning it just wasn't there any more.

MRS. C. You know I could have lived my whole life without knowing that Wilson.

D.L. Here let me give you some money, *(She hands him bills out of her purse.)* and when you've got the flowers, would you bring them to my room please, I'd like to write a note and deliver them personally.

(Exits room 8.)

MRS. C. Did you hook this phone up?

WILSON. Yeah, just finished.

MRS. C. Well, does it work?

WILSON. I dunno. She told me to hook it up, not test it. Anyway there's wires all over the place down there. *(The counter phone rings.)* There you go, it's working.

MRS. C. *(Picks up the phone.)* Reception. Hello. You want to know what? How much weight is Golden Girl carrying? I wouldn't have thought it would have been any of your business. What? I don't care if you do want your usual on Love Goddess to show at 5 o'clock. You can't have it, not in my club. Good day sir. *(Slams the phone down.)* Wilson!

WILSON. I know, I know, the wires are crossed again.

(DAVID has come out of the bathroom of room 13, exited to the hallway, closed the door, and come down to the reception desk. He carries a putter and a golf ball.)

MRS. C. Everything alright Mr. McGachen?

DAVID. Just fine thank you. I noticed the putting green out front, and I thought I'd just get a little practice till Mr. Baker gets back.

WILSON. You going to be playing a round with Mr. Baker are you?

DAVID. Well we were going to but something came up.

(WILSON raises he eyes heavenward.)

MRS. C. What's wrong with you?

WILSON. Funny you should ask, you see I've got these shooting pains, they start in my kneecaps and—

MRS. C. Wilson! *(To DAVID.)* Don't pay any attention to him. *(To WILSON.)* Don't you have an errand to run?

WILSON. I've told you I don't run anywhere. *(MRS. C. opens her mouth to say something.)* Alright, alright. I'm going. *(He exits to the front entrance muttering to himself.)* Roses, for the couple in room 3, so romantic. I don't believe it—

DAVID. What on earth is he talking about?

MRS. C. Oh don't take any notice of him, he seems to be in one of his moods today. Excuse me.

(Exits to office. DAVID takes a step L. and practices a putting stroke, as D.L. enters from room 8. She turns, as if to go R. on the landing, sees DAVID and comes D. to his R.)

D.L. Ah Mr. McGachen. I hope you're not planning on playing golf without your wife.

DAVID. No, no. Definitely not! She's—er—still shopping. I thought I'd just wait for her on the putting green.

D.L. Good. I can't tell you how much I'm looking forward to meeting her.

(JOHN enters from the front entrance. He is carrying a box-like package and a large plastic shopping bag. D.L., who is facing L. and slightly D.S. of DAVID, does not see him. DAVID puts his L. hand out, palm forward towards JOHN, to signal him to stop and get out, which he does. D.L. looks strangely at DAVID, who then flips his hand backward and forward, as though examining his nails.)

DAVID. I simply must get a manicure, it's been far too long.
D.L. *(Frowning.)* Really? Well, I'll see you about six then.

(Exits R. on the landing. DAVID comes D.R. and signals to JOHN to come in.)

JOHN. Was that her?
DAVID. Yes. That was close. *(He goes up the steps and looks R. on the landing.)* O.K. come on, she's gone. Did you get everything?

JOHN. *(Follows him up.)* Yes, but are you sure you want me to do this?

(They both enter room 11.)

DAVID. I'm more convinced than ever. She's definitely going to fire me if I don't produce a wife.

JOHN. O.K. but let's try to keep it short and sweet. I meet her, one drink and I'm gone.

(He picks up the suitcase from the bed and goes into the bathroom, leaving the door open.)

DAVID. That should do it.

JOHN. *(Off.)* I wonder what D.L. stands for?

DAVID. Dragon Lady I should think.

JOHN. *(Off.)* Remind me to tell her you said that.

DAVID. Sure. Listen, while you're getting ready, I'm going to move the car round and check out the pro shop. I haven't given up on golf yet.

JOHN. *(Off.)* Well I have. Just as soon as we've had one drink with the dragon lady, I'm out of here.

(DAVID exits room 11, closes the door, and goes R. as the phones on the counter and the table both ring. TINA enters from the office and picks up the phone on the counter.)

TINA. Oakfield Golf and Country Club—Little green man? No I can't—(The table phone continues to ring.) Oh good grief! *(DAVID has come down the steps, so she hands him the counter phone.)* Could you hold this for me for a second please? *(DAVID takes the phone and listens as TINA crosses L. and picks up the phone on the table.)* Oakfield Golf and Country Club, yes, oh—reservations. Just a moment please, I have to get to the computer. *(She heads R. to the office.)* You can hang that up, it's a wrong number.

(TINA exits to the office. DAVID hangs up the counter phone, but it rings again immediately. He picks it up.)

DAVID. Hello. Who is this? The Oakfield Golf and Country Club? Just a minute. *(He calls to the office door.)* Miss! *(TINA appears in the doorway with a phone to her ear.)* You've got another call.

TINA. I know, it's me.
DAVID. You mean—
TINA. We're talking to each other.

(She disappears for a moment into the office.)

DAVID. ... I thought you sounded familiar.

(TINA reappears and crosses L. to the table phone.)

TINA. One moment please madam. *(To DAVID.)* Here hold this.

(She hands him the table phone, reaching with it across the couch, and signals to DAVID to reach as far as he can with the other phone. The two cords fail to meet by about two feet. DAVID ends up stretched over the R. end of the couch, the table phone in his left hand, and the counter phone in his right. By leaning, first one way, and then the other, he can use both phones at once.)

DAVID. *(To table phone.)* We're checking your reservation now madam.

(TINA runs into the office and reappears immediately with the office phone to her ear. The cord is just long enough to enable her to be seen in the office doorway.)

TINA. *(Into the phone.)* May I have your name please?
DAVID. *(Leaning R.)* I'm David McGachen.
TINA. No, no, the other phone.
DAVID. Oh I see. *(Leaning L. to the table phone.)* May I have your name please? Mrs. Faraday.
TINA. What?
DAVID. *(Leaning R.)* Mrs. Faraday.
TINA. I need a date of arrival and the number of days she'll be staying.

(WILSON, unseen by TINA or DAVID, has entered from the front en-

*trance. He is carrying a bouquet of roses in a vase. He stops
dead in his tracks as he hears:)*

DAVID. May I have a date Mrs. Faraday? *(WILSON, mouths the
word "date" toward the audience and backs away R. to listen. He
remains visible, extreme D.S.R. in the front entrance.)* Do I have a
king size bed? *(WILSON reacts, DAVID looks at TINA who nods.)*
Yes I do. I see, you want to start on the 14th and stay in the room for
three weeks. *(WILSON reacts, TINA nods her approval.)* I'm sure I
can manage that. You want to play a round every day? *(He looks
questioningly at TINA who nods.)* No problem. Twice a day if you
feel up to it. *(TINA nods again.)* Absolutely. Oh I agree. I like to get
started early in the morning myself. *(WILSON continues to react.)* I'll
look forward to having you on the fourteenth. Thank you Mrs. Faraday.

*He puts the table phone down on the couch, goes R. to hang up the
counter phone then back L. to hang up the table phone. TINA
goes into the office to hang up the office phone, but reappears
immediately as WILSON enters.)*

WILSON. I don't believe it! Three weeks, twice a day. I don't
know where you get the staying power.
DAVID. What did you say?
WILSON. I said why don't you say it with flowers?

He holds up the vase.)

TINA. Thanks for your help Mr. McGachen, you saved my life.
DAVID. You're welcome. See you later.

Exits front entrance.)

TINA. These phones are still all screwed up. Can't you do anything?
WILSON. I don't think so. Let me get rid of these flowers and I'll
give it another try.

(He goes up and knocks on the door of room 8.)

    D.L. *(Opens the door.)* That was quick, oh they're beautiful. *(Takes the vase.)* Thank you Wilson, did you have enough money?
    WILSON. Just barely.
    D.L. I see. Just a minute.

(She goes back into room 8.)

    TINA.   You're terrible, you know that.
    WILSON. I have to do it, it's all these doctor bills.
    D.L. *(Reappears in the doorway with a bill in her hand which she gives to WILSON, and a card which she puts in the flowers.)* Here you are, thank you Wilson.

(She closes the door of room 8 and goes L. on the landing.)

    WILSON. Thank you. *(He comes D. to TINA who is still behind the counter.)* There's another one of those old junction boxes in the office. Maybe I could have a look at that.

(Exits to the office, followed by TINA.
D.L. knocks on the door of room 13. JOHN comes out of the bath room of room 11. He is wearing the wig and make-up, but is still in his regular clothes. He moves through the connecting door.)

    JOHN. Who is it?
    D.L. *(Off.)* It's me, D.L. Hutchison.
    JOHN. *(Panics for a moment and starts back to room 11, realizes that won't work, comes back to room 13 and closes the connecting door.)* Just a minute. *(He looks frantically around for something to cover himself. He takes a cover from the bed and drapes it over himself, looks at his trouser bottoms and shoes, puts the cover back on the bed. Then, in desperation, jumps into bed and holds the covers up to his chin.)* Come in.
    D.L. *(Enters holding the flowers.)* Oh, please forgive me. I didn't mean to disturb you. You must be Mrs. McGachen.

JOHN. *(In a high voice.)* Yes. Hello.

D.L. I'm D.L. Hutchison, your husband's new president.

JOHN. How do you do?

(He carefully manages to get one hand out from under the covers, and they shake hands.)

D.L. Does your husband know you're here? I think he's out front waiting for you.

JOHN. Oh, well you see I was simply exhausted from shopping, so I came straight to our room for a little nap.

D.L. Well, don't let me disturb you. I brought you two love birds some flowers, and I wrote a little note, just to let you know how the new Ashley Maureen Corporation feels about families who spend their leisure time together.

JOHN. *(Takes the flowers with one hand, using the other to keep the covers up to his chin, and puts them on the bedside table.)* Thank you very much. *(There is a pause, JOHN smiles sweetly at D.L. and primps his hair.)* So you're Miss Hutchison?

D.L. Mrs. actually, but please call me D.L. everyone does.

JOHN. O.K. D.L. it is. I'm Karly.

D.L. Well, perhaps I should let you rest Karly, we're all getting together for cocktails about six.

JOHN. I'll look forward to that.

D.L. Good. It's been so nice meeting you. I'll see you a little later then.

(She exits room 13, closes the door and goes into room 8.)

JOHN. *(Watches her go, then gets out of bed, looks at the flowers.)* Love birds!

(He goes into room 11, leaving the connecting door open, drops the wig on the bed, and exits to bathroom 11. The counter phone rings and MRS. CARLSON enters from the office to answer it.)

MRS. C. Good afternoon, Oakfield Golf and Country Club. What do you mean "on the nose"? We don't have a little green man. *(The table phone rings, she pushes open the office door and calls in.)* Tina! *(TINA enters immediately and MRS. C. gestures to the other phone. TINA crosses L. to answer it.)* Just who is this please?

TINA. Good afternoon, Oakfield Golf and Country Club, what? Wilson? Where are you? *(WILSON appears in the doorway of the office with a phone to his ear.)* Oh!

WILSON. Sorry everyone. I'll try some different wires.

(He returns to the office as TINA hangs up.)

MRS. C. What do you mean, "can I get it on for you?" I haven't the remotest idea what you're talking about, but I feel supremely confident when I tell you that, not today, not tomorrow, not at any time can I "get it on for you". Good day sir! *(Hangs up the phone with a bang.)* These phones are driving me insane, can't Wilson do anything about them?

TINA. He's trying, but I wouldn't hold your breath if I were you.

MRS. C. Oh well. Tell you what, why don't you take off a little early. It seems pretty quiet.

TINA. Thank you. You sure you can manage?

MRS. C. I'm just fine. Wilson is on till 8 o'clock if I need any help.

TINA. O.K. Let me get my things, and I'm out of here.

(Exits to office. JOHN, in regular clothes and without make-up, has come out of the bathroom in room 11, and exited room 11 to the hallway. He comes D. towards the reception desk.)

MRS. C. Is everything alright Mr. Baker?

JOHN. Everything is just fine thank you. Have you seen Mr McGachen?

MRS. C. Well, not since you checked in. *(Enter D.L. from room 8. She comes D.)* Ah, Mrs. Hutchison, *(JOHN hurriedly turns away so as not to be seen by D.L. then moves quickly L., sits in the chair and holds up the newspaper so D.L. can't see his face.)* Everything al right?

D.L. Fine thanks.

MRS. C. It's almost like an Ashley Maureen convention here this weekend.

D.L. What?

MRS. C. Well, there's you of course, and then there's Mr. McGachen in room 13 and Mr. Baker in room 11 here to play golf this weekend. *(The office phone rings.)* That's the office phone. Excuse me.

(Exits to office.)

D.L. *(Comes right up to JOHN.)* Mr. John Baker?

JOHN. *(Lowers the paper.)* Yes, that's me.

D.L. I'm D.L. Hutchison.

JOHN. *(Stands)* How do you do?

(They shake hands.)

D.L. You know, you look very familiar. Have we met before?

JOHN. I don't think so.

D.L. *(Frowning, and just a little hesitant.)* No, we couldn't have. Well I'm delighted to meet you now Mr. Baker.

JOHN. Oh the pleasure is all mine D.L.

D.L. Ah-ha! The files said you were a smooth talker.

JOHN. Files?

D.L. The personnel files.

JOHN. Oh, I see.

D.L. So, you're here to play golf with Mr. McGachen are you?

JOHN. *(Quickly.)* Yes, but my wife is here too.

D.L. She is?

JOHN. Oh yes. She went shopping, but now she's back.

D.L. Excellent, I just get such a good feeling about an executive who spends his time off with his wife. I'll look forward to meeting her.

JOHN. Meeting her?

D.L. Absolutely.

JOHN. Oh dear.

D.L. Pardon me?
JOHN. I said "she's here".

(TINA enters from the office, dressed as before, but wearing a suit type jacket and carrying a purse. She heads for the front entrance.)

D.L. Oh?
JOHN. Yes she's here. Right here. This is my wife, Tina.

(He crosses R., grabs TINA, and pushes her towards D.L., who puts out a hand.)

TINA. Who? What?
D.L. *(Grabs TINA's hand and shakes it.)* How do you do Mrs Baker?
TINA. Mrs. Baker?
D.L. I'm delighted to meet you.
TINA. I'm not Mrs. Baker.
JOHN. *(Steps forward and puts his arm around TINA's shoulders.)* Of course you are my darling. Now that we're married your name is Baker. She hasn't got used to her new name. *(There is a brief pause as everyone looks at JOHN.)* You see we just got married today.
TINA. We did?
D.L. But the files said you've been married to Laura for nine years.
JOHN. Ah, yes, well—that was my first marriage.
D.L. First marriage?
JOHN. Yes.
D.L. What happened to your first wife?
JOHN. *(Quickly.)* She died.
D.L. I'm sorry. I didn't know. I guess the files really aren't up to date.
JOHN. Yes, that must be it. *(TINA pushes JOHN D.S.R. a little and opens her mouth to say something.)* Just go along with it please.
D.L. What did you say?

JOHN. I said my first wife got a disease.

D.L. Oh how terrible. What?

JOHN. What what?

D.L. What disease did she die of?

TINA. *(Aside to JOHN.)* You're nuts, you know that, and when the men in little white coats come to take you away I'll testify—

JOHN. That's it. Tsetse fly! She was bitten by a tsetse fly.

D.L. In Connecticut?

JOHN. Er—er—we were on vacation in Costa Rica.

D.L. How very sad. Still we mustn't dwell on the past, and as I won't be seeing you next week—

JOHN. Why won't you be seeing me next week?

D.L. Well, you're on your honeymoon.

JOHN. Ah, yes. But I'll be at work on Monday morning.

D.L. Really? Now that's what I call a company man. Alright then, why don't I meet you both here about six, we can have a drink before dinner and get to know each other.

JOHN. Couldn't it be earlier?

D.L. I really don't think we should be drinking cocktails before 6 o'clock. That's something I wouldn't like to see in my executives. I hope it's not a habit of yours.

JOHN. No, no of course not. Let's make it later then, a lot later.

D.L. No, six is good. Then we can all have dinner together. After all, you are on your honeymoon and we mustn't keep you up too late. Anyway, Mr. and Mrs. McGachen will be joining us. Well, I've got to go and arrange some golf lessons. See you all later.

(Exits U.L. on the landing.)

JOHN. *(Watches her go, then turns to TINA.)* Thank you.

TINA. Why did you tell her we were married?

JOHN. It's a long story.

TINA. Well make it short, I'm done for the day and I'm on my way home.

JOHN. Oh dear, you've just got to stay and see it through.

TINA. Mr. Baker, I have no idea what's going on here, but let me assure you of one thing, I haven't got to do anything.

JOHN. Of course not. I'm sorry. I didn't mean it like that. It's just that I'm desperate. I really need you to pretend to be my wife for a little while.

TINA. For heaven's sake, why?

JOHN. Because if I don't produce a wife by six o'clock, the dragon lady will fire me.

TINA. Listen, I'd like to help, I really would, but you're not making any sense.

JOHN. Tell you what. How would you like a car full of Ashley Maureen cosmetic samples?

TINA. A car full?

JOHN. Two cars full—a lifetime supply.

TINA. What exactly would I have to do?

JOHN. Be my wife for about an hour. Now let's get the first of the samples out of my car while I tell you all about it. You see this D.L. Hutchison woman....

(They exit, talking, to the front entrance. The table phone rings. MRS. CARLSON enters from the office, crosses L. and picks it up.)

MRS. C. Oakfield Golf and Country Club. What? No. I don't care who you are, you may not put a big one on Love Goddess at five o'clock, and it is absolutely out of the question for you to roll anything over at five-thirty. *(She hangs up abruptly.)* Wilson!

(WILSON enters from the office as D.L. and DAVID enter from U.L. on the landing.)

D.L. I feel I'm getting to know you already. Ah, Mrs. Carlson, wonder if I could get some room service please?

MRS. C. Of course. Our receptionist has left for the day, but Wilson will be happy to oblige. Won't you Wilson?

(WILSON raises his eyebrows to the heavens.)

D.L. Thank you. I'd like a bottle of your very best champagne sent to room 11 with my compliments.

DAVID. Room 11?

MRS. C. Room 11?

D.L. Yes, for the honeymooners.

DAVID. In Room 11?

MRS. C. Honeymooners?

D.L. Yes, why didn't you tell me Mr. and Mrs. Baker were here?

DAVID. Mrs. Baker?

MRS. C. Mrs. Baker?

D.L. Yes, she's such a pretty little thing don't you think?

WILSON. *(To no one in particular.)* I don't believe it. Now there's three of them. And I thought I'd seen it all.

MRS. C. Wilson, please try again with the phones. I'll get the champagne myself, Mrs. Hutchison.

(WILSON exits to the office shaking his head. MRS. CARLSON exits to the front entrance.)

DAVID. You've met Mr. Baker?

D.L. Yes, and Mrs. Baker. I've asked them to join us for cocktails at six.

DAVID. Us?

D.L. Yes, you and your wife. You do remember don't you?

DAVID. How could I ever forget?

D.L. You know I really am quite impressed with Mr. Baker.

DAVID. You are?

D.L. Yes, such devotion to duty. Just think, newly married, and he's planning on being at work on Monday morning— *(Enter JOHN and TINA from the front entrance.)* —and speaking of devotion here are the little love birds.

JOHN. Ah, D.L. You're still here. David! Nice to see you old buddy. You remember my wife, Tina, don't you? Of course you do, well we were just going up to our room to get changed before dinner. Weren't we my precious?

TINA. Room? Changed? You didn't say anything about that. I'm not sure—

JOHN. Bless her, she's a little shy. Come along my little turtle-love.

TINA. I'm having second thoughts about this. I don't think —
JOHN. *(Takes TINA by the elbow and steers her U.S.)* Nothing's
going to happen, come my angel. We'll see you about six D.L.

(JOHN and TINA exit U.L. then into room 11.)

D.L. Right. That's a good idea. I need to freshen up myself. I'll
see you at six Mr. McGachen.

*(Exits room 8. DAVID watches her go, then rushes U.L. as WILSON
puts his head out of the office door. He has obviously been listening. He follows DAVID and exits U.L. on the landing.)*

JOHN. *(Follows TINA into room 11 and closes the door.)* I can
assure you I'm not here for any "hanky panky" as you put it. In half an
hour or so, it'll all be over and you'll be on your way home.
TINA. O.K., O.K. I believe you. It was just that when you said
we were going to our room to change, it sounded real kinky.
JOHN. I'm sorry.
TINA. It's O.K. Mind if I use the bathroom?

(Exits to bathroom.)

DAVID. *(Has now entered room 13, leaving the door open, and
come into room 11.)* What the hell is going on here?
JOHN. Calm down, calm down. I can explain everything.

(WILSON is now seen in the doorway of room 13, listening.)

DAVID. Go right ahead "old buddy".
JOHN. Look David, everything is going to be alright. I bumped
into D.L., and just like you, I had to produce a wife, and Tina sort of
volunteered.

(WILSON takes a step into the room straining to hear.)

DAVID. She's your wife?

JOHN. And I'm her husband.

DAVID. But you can't be her husband. You're married to me!

(WILSON reacts, turns to the audience with eyes bulging, mouths the words "I don't believe it" then returns to the office.)

JOHN. I'm sorry, but it was all I could think of at the time.

DAVID. We're not dead yet. We've still got fifteen minutes to find another wife for me.

JOHN. Oh Lord!

DAVID. Now what?

JOHN. I'd forgotten. D.L. has already met your wife.

DAVID. You mean she's here?

JOHN. Not exactly.

DAVID. What are you talking about?

JOHN. *(Picks up the wig from the bed, puts it on, and in a high voice:)* "Hello D.L."

DAVID. She's seen you?

JOHN. *(Takes the wig off.)* I'm sorry David, it's over.

DAVID. It's not over till the fat lady sings. Let me think.

JOHN. If you say so, but to me it looks like the orchestra's playing and the fat lady is on her feet with her mouth wide open.

DAVID. I've got it!

JOHN. What?

DAVID. The fat lady has laryngitis. Listen to this. D.L. doesn't ever meet both of you at the same time.

JOHN. What?

DAVID. We can do it. We meet D.L. for drinks at six, just as we originally planned.

JOHN. Who's we?

DAVID. Me and you. That is me and my wife.

JOHN. What about me and my wife?

DAVID. You'll be late. After a few minutes as my wife, you excuse yourself to go to the bathroom, and a couple of minutes later Mr. and Mrs. Baker arrive.

JOHN. Then what?

DAVID. We chat for a while, then you excuse yourself and come back as my wife.

JOHN. Just how long do you think we can keep that up?

DAVID. Yeah. That's right. Let me think.

JOHN. I hear the fat lady!

DAVID. Not yet you don't. At some point you—that is my wife—gets sick or something and has to make her excuses, then you can spend the rest of the evening as John Baker.

JOHN. I'm not that good David, it'll never work.

DAVID. I think you are that good, and I think we can get away with it. Now, what about Tina?

JOHN. What about her?

DAVID. Why is she doing this?

JOHN. I promised her a lifetime supply of Ashley Maureen cosmetics. I've just put all I had with me in her car.

DAVID. No, what I meant was *(Enter TINA from the bathroom.)* does she know you're going to be my wife?

TINA. Hold it right there you guys. This has gone far enough. I'm out of here.

(She comes D. to the foot of the bed and starts to cross L. DAVID and JOHN grab her and all three sit at the foot of the bed.)

JOHN. Please, it's not what you think. You know how I explained about D.L. and wives? Well it's the same thing for David here.

TINA. What?

DAVID. John, you've got to get changed. We've only got about five minutes. Tina, why don't you come with me. I've got a ton-load of samples in my car, and while we load them into yours, I'll explain about who my wife is.

TINA. O.K. But you'd better make it good.

DAVID. John, for heaven's sake, don't just stand there, get going.

(JOHN exits to the bathroom of room 11, taking the wig with him. DAVID and TINA exit room 11, closing the door, and go R. on the landing. Enter MRS. CARLSON from the front entrance, car

rying a bottle of champagne, she heads for the office but stops just as she gets behind the counter.)

MRS. C. Oh good grief, look at all these wires.

(She puts the champagne down on the counter and bends down out of sight, as DAVID and TINA come down and make their way to the front entrance.)

DAVID. So you see, once she had seen him it was too late to swap wives, but as long as my wife and your husband are never in the same room together, we should be able to pull it off. Now here's how it will work. Half way through the evening, John will swap and become your husband for a while. Just remember, you're on your honeymoon in room 11, and we're in room 13. With a bit of luck she'll never know...

They exit the front entrance.)

MRS. C. *(Stands up, her eyes bulging.)* We'll see about that, wife swapping indeed! Not in my club. Wilson!
WILSON. *(Enters from the office.)* Yeah?
MRS. C. Do you know who are in rooms 11 and 13?
WILSON. Those guys from the make-up company.
MRS. C. That's right. It was room 11 that Mrs. Hutchison ordered the champagne for. *(With a sudden realization.)* O-o-o-h! On their honeymoon! It's depraved, that's what it is. Champagne indeed! I think not. Wilson, *(She hands him the bottle.)* put this in the office, we cannot condone this sort of behavior.
WILSON. Oh, so you've found out about those two huh?
MRS. C. Indeed I have, and I intend to put a stop to it.
WILSON. Just how do you propose to do that?
MRS. C. I intend to catch them and demand that they leave this club. In the meantime, what I want you to do, is fix these wretched phones.
WILSON. I'm working on it, I'm working on it. I'd go faster but all this bending down is bad for my lumbago and —

MRS. C. Thank you Wilson.

(He exits to the office.
Enter D.L. from room 8, dressed as before, but without her suit
jacket.)

D.L. Ah Mrs. Carlson, did you deliver the champagne to room 11?

(D.L. comes D.)

MRS. C. I most certainly did not.

D.L. I beg your pardon.

MRS. C. Mrs. Hutchison, are you aware of what is going on in
room 11?

D.L. I'm not sure I know exactly what you mean.

MRS. C. It has come to my attention that there are sexual shenanigans taking place.

D.L. *(Laughing.)* Sexual shenanigans?

MRS. C. I don't see any reason for laughter.

D.L. Well isn't that what honeymoons are for?

MRS. C. Oh!

(She storms into the office.)
D.L. crosses L., sits in the chair and picks up the newspaper, as
DAVID and TINA enter from the front entrance.)

DAVID. You should have at least a year's supply of pretty much
everything—ah D.L., *(Looks at his watch.)* good heavens, it's almost
six. I'll just go and see if Mrs. McGachen is ready.

D.L. Good. As a matter of fact, I would like to have a private
word with Mrs. Baker.

TINA. You would?

D.L. Yes my dear, why don't you sit down?

(TINA looks at DAVID in panic.)

DAVID. I'll be as quick as I can.

D.L. Take your time. There's no hurry. *(DAVID goes U., exits L. on the landing, goes into room 11, closing the door, and into the bathroom. TINA sits on the sofa, D.L. is L. on the chair.)* Now my dear, I couldn't help but notice a little earlier how nervous you were about your wedding night. *(TINA opens her mouth to say something, but D.L. presses on.)* So I take it that you and Mr. Baker have—er— how do I put this delicately,—er—not—er—you know, haven't—

TINA. No we definitely haven't, and we're not going to either.

(JOHN, now in wig, dress, make-up, etc., and DAVID come out of the bathroom of room 11, exit room 11, closing the door, and go R. on the landing.)

D.L. Oh dear, you really are nervous about tonight aren't you. You know, I think I shall insist that your husband does not come to work on Monday. It's important that you two have a little more time together. *(JOHN and DAVID come down.)* Mrs. McGachen, how nice to see you again.

JOHN. Hello.

(They all sit. D.L. on the chair L. TINA on the couch L. end. JOHN on the couch R. end. DAVID on the couch R. arm. JOHN sits in an ungainly position with his legs and knees apart. His right ankle on his left knee. DAVID sees this and quickly pushes JOHN's right knee over to the left and down, so JOHN's legs are now crossed. This produces a silent scream and a look of excruciating pain on JOHN's face.)

DAVID. We were just chatting about how nice it is for both of us to have the opportunity to meet you informally like this D.L., before we all get down to work next week.

D.L. You're right of course, but I was just saying to Mrs. Baker that perhaps her husband shouldn't come in next week.

JOHN. Oh, why not?

TINA. She wants us to have a longer honeymoon.

D.L. The new marriage needs to get off on a solid foundation. I'm not sure if any of us can really understand what Mr. Baker must have gone through at the time of the tragic death of his first wife.

DAVID. His first wife?

TINA. His first wife.

DAVID. Dead?

TINA. Dead.

JOHN. Yes dear, surely you remember?

TINA. Don't you remember, she got bitten by a tsetse fly.

DAVID. A tsetse fly?

JOHN. Yes.

DAVID. In Connecticut?

TINA. They were on vacation in Costa Rica.

DAVID. I've never heard of anything so—

JOHN. *(Jumping in, grabbing the front of his shirt, and glowering at DAVID.)* Tragic!

DAVID. What? Oh right. Tragic, very tragic.

D.L. So tell me a little about yourself Mrs. McGachen.

JOHN. Oh there's nothing to tell really, I lead a very ordinary life.

D.L. Oh come now, I'm sure there's something you could surprise me with.

WILSON. *(Enters from the office, with tools and wires in his hand, just in time to hear the last sentence.)* Oh he could surprise you alright.

D.L. What?

WILSON. I said it looks like these wires are too tight.

(Bends down out of sight.)

DAVID. My wife is right D.L. We don't get out much, our main interest is the company of course.

D.L. Of course.

JOHN. You know D.L., I'm sure that's true of John as well. David is always telling me that John's success is due to his total sincerity.

D.L. Really David? That's quite a compliment, coming from a fellow worker.

DAVID. Oh yes, he's always sincere, whether he means it or not.

but he's really a deeply superficial person.

JOHN. *(Interrupts quickly.)* Good heavens, its five after six already. I wonder where your husband is Tina. It's not like him to be late. As a matter of fact, one of John's greatest assets is his punctuality. If he's late, I bet it's because he's found a new sales rep or something. He never stops you know. He's a real company man. At least that's what David always tells me. *(DAVID is glaring at JOHN.)* Well, if you'll excuse me, I have to use the little girls room.

(WILSON stands up momentarily, raises his eyebrows, mouths the words "I don't believe it" to the audience, then bends down out of sight again. JOHN nudges TINA.)

TINA. Oh, right. Why don't I come with you, and I'll see if I can find my husband.

(JOHN and TINA exit U.L. on the landing, then into room 11. JOHN goes into the bathroom, hurriedly starting to change, as TINA sits on the bed.)

D.L. Your wife is very charming David. I wonder if perhaps she might be able to help the Bakers with their little problem.

DAVID. *(Sits on couch L. end.)* What problem is that D.L.?

D.L. Well, as you know, this is their wedding night and Mrs. Baker seems—er—how shall I put this—er—reluctant to perform her wifely duties.

DAVID. *(Laughing.)* Wifely duties?

D.L.. I see nothing humorous in this Mr. McGachen. We must all help to put her at ease. *(WILSON stands up fiddling with wires.)* The champagne will definitely help her to relax. *(Sees WILSON.)* Did we ever get that champagne Wilson?

WILSON. Yes, but Mrs. Carlson had me put it in the office.

D.L. Well, as soon as you've finished what you're doing, would you please deliver it to room 11.

WILSON. Just as soon as I've finished with these phones, and the muscle spasms in my back have quieted down, I'll be right on it.

D.L. Thank you Wilson. I've written a little card, would you deliver this with it please. *(She gets up, crosses R. to WILSON and hands him the card. He takes the card and exits to the office. D.L. returns to her chair. JOHN, now in regular clothes, has come out of the bathroom of room 11. He and TINA exit room 11, go R. on the landing and a moment later, come down and sit on the couch. TINA R. end, JOHN on the arm.)* Now, we can play our part too—

JOHN. Sorry I'm late D.L. I got a little tied up with the beauty parlor manager. I've just about convinced her to carry our products. I don't like to miss any opportunity. Yes ma'am that's me. On the job day and night. Isn't that right dear?

TINA. Oh yes, he never stops. He's a real company man alright.

D.L. I'm sure we all appreciate that John, but on your honeymoon?

JOHN. Sorry about that D.L., it's hard to break old habits you know.

D.L. Yes but now that you're married, and there's two of you again, you need to tread carefully to avoid hurting the feelings of your new bride.

DAVID. We all need to tread carefully to avoid stepping in all this stuff he's spreading around.

JOHN. I can honestly tell you D.L. that my first thought in the morning, and my last thought at night, is the company.

DAVID. Good God, we're up to our knees in it.

D.L. What was that?

JOHN. He meant the Company. We're very pleased with it.

D.L. Oh I see, good, good.

DAVID. Believe me, my friend here, from outer space, and I are delighted to be here.

D.L. Excellent. As soon as Mrs. McGachen gets back, I thought we might all have a drink on that lovely little terrace that overlooks the eighteenth green.

DAVID. Terrific idea D.L.

D.L. You know, I think I'll just get my jacket, it might be a little chilly out there.

(She gets up and exits to room 8. They all stand in silence and watch her go.)

JOHN. Now what?

DAVID. One more quick change and then you say you're not feeling well, and you've got to go to the room to lie down. That's the last anyone sees of you as my wife. The rest of the evening you're John Baker, and we're home free. Hurry now.

(John rushes U.L. on the landing, into room 11 and in to the bathroom.)

TINA. What about me?

DAVID. We need you to stay, at least for a little while, please.

TINA. She's going to start asking me questions. I know she is.

DAVID. Alright, listen. We'll go on the terrace and have a drink, and when John says he's not feeling well, and wants to go and lie down, you can say you'd better go with him, and then you can go home. How's that?

TINA. It's O.K. I guess, but I've just got a feeling something is going to go wrong. *(The counter phone rings. TINA picks it up.)* Reception, hello, hello.

(She presses buttons and suddenly a voice comes over the loud speakers.)

VOICE. Hello.

TINA. Oh dear!

(She's frantically pushing buttons.)

VOICE. Hello.

TINA. Hello, can I help you?

VOICE. I'm sure you can darling. I was told I could get some action at this number.

TINA. Could you speak a little more quietly please, everybody seems to be able to hear you.

VOICE. *(Confidentially.)* Sure, I understand. Now listen darling, what I want to know is this. Has there been any activity this afternoon on Baker's Man?

TINA. No, and there isn't going to be any either.

VOICE. That's funny. I had a hot tip that Baker's Man was getting ready to make a surprise move today.

TINA. Who told you that?

VOICE. I'm afraid that's a bit confidential darling.

TINA. Well let me tell you, that if he makes any sort of move, I'll be on him like a ton of bricks.

VOICE. That's the spirit. You know, you sound like my sort of girl. I could really go for you.

TINA. I'm sure I meet all your requirements. After all I am breathing.

VOICE. Don't be like that. Tell you what, I'm going to check the other runners and get back to you. Bye darling.

(TINA hangs up, as D.L. enters from room 8, now wearing her suit jacket. She comes D.)

D.L. Where is everyone?

TINA. My husband went to get some samples for the beauty parlor.

(She grins at DAVID, very proud of herself.)

DAVID. My wife went to get an aspirin, she's not feeling too well. *(JOHN, now in female attire again, comes out of bathroom 11 rushes out of room 11, leaving the door open, and comes D.)* Ah, here she is now. Feeling a little better darling?

JOHN. Yes, thank you darling.

D.L. We'd better not wait for Mr. Baker. I'm sure he'll find us on the terrace. Shall we?

(They all exit U.R. on the landing, as WILSON enters from the office. He carries the champagne in an ice bucket, two glasses and D. L.'s card on a small tray. He goes up to room 11. He taps on the open door, no one answers so he enters, puts the tray on the bed side table, props up the card, then comes D. and exits to the office as LAURA BAKER and KARLY McGACHEN enter from the

front entrance. LAURA is a pretty little thing in her mid-thirties. Not a very forceful character, as we shall see, she tends rather to "go with the flow" and cries at the drop of a hat. KARLY, age perhaps 40, is, on the other hand, much more the take charge type. Both are dressed smartly, but conservatively, and each carry two large shopping bags, and a small overnight case. They come up to the counter, dump all the bags on the floor, and KARLY rings the call bell. MRS. CARLSON enters immediately.)

MRS. C. Good evening, may I help you?

KARLY. Good evening. I'm Mrs. Karly McGachen and this is Mrs. Laura Baker. I believe our husbands have already checked in.

MRS. C. Mrs. McGachen?

KARLY. Yes.

MRS. C. And Mrs. Baker?

LAURA. Yes.

MRS. C. I see.

(There is a slight pause.)

KARLY. We'd like to join our husbands in their rooms please.

MRS. C. They booked two single rooms.

LAURA. Oh that's alright. They really weren't expecting us. We got kind of bored shopping and decided to surprise them. So you can just change the rooms to doubles.

MRS. C. I'm sure I can. You're lucky. We are very quiet this weekend. In addition to your—er—"husbands" we only have one other guest, a D.L. Hutchison, so you see I am able to provide you with separate rooms.

KARLY. Thank you, but we would prefer to be with our husbands.

MRS. C. I see. Very well, and which of you would be in which room?

LAURA. I beg your pardon.

MRS. C. Well now, let's see. Mr. McGachen is in room 13, and Mr. Baker is in room 11, though I don't suppose you care who is in which room do you?

    LAURA. What in heaven's name are you talking about?

    KARLY. Oh come on. Have you got someone to carry our bags please?

    MRS. C. *(Opens the office door a fraction and calls in.)* Wilson!

    KARLY. Thank you.

(WILSON enters.)

    MRS. C. Wilson, would you help these—er—*(She pauses and looks at them.)* ladies with their bags please.

    WILSON. You know my arthritis is really playing up today, and at my age—

    MRS. C. Wilson!

    WILSON. I know, I know. What's the room numbers?

    MRS. C. Eleven and thirteen.

(She hands him keys.)

    WILSON. *(Stops dead in his tracks.)* Two more? You know, it's times like this when I feel I missed a whole generation somewhere.

(He picks up the two cases and heads U.)

    KARLY. *(She and LAURA pick up the shopping bags.)* Come on it's going to be so much fun to surprise them.

    WILSON. *(Turns D.S.)* I don't think you've really got any idea just how much fun it's going to be!

    MRS. C. I want you to know that this club enjoys a spotless reputation, and I consider it my duty to protect that reputation. I will not have anyone lowering those standards by raising their skirts. I will therefore be paying particular attention to making sure that nothing abnormal takes place this weekend.

(She wheels about, and exits to the office with a flourish.)

    KARLY. The only abnormal thing about this place is her.

(WILSON has gone on ahead, and now appears in the doorway of room 11, holding LAURA's case. He is followed by LAURA.)

WILSON. Here you are Mrs. Baker.

(She reaches for the case, but WILSON, who is not about to surrender it until he has received a tip, simply clutches it more firmly.)

LAURA. Oh, I see. *(She gives him a tip.)* Thank you Wilson.
WILSON. Thank you ma-am. *(He gives her the case and turns to KARLY who is right behind him.)* Now you're right next door Mrs. McGachen.

(He closes the door of room 11, and they reappear momentarily in the door of room 13. He is once again carrying KARLY's case.)

KARLY. *(Steps past him into the room.)* Thank you Wilson. *(He just stands there.)* Oh!

(She searches in her purse and hands him a tip.)

WILSON. Thank you, ma'am.

(Puts the case down. He closes the door of room 13, goes R. on the landing, comes D., and exits to the office. LAURA puts her shopping bags in the bathroom, comes back out and closes the bathroom door. She then sees the champagne on the bedside table, picks up the note and reads it. KARLY puts her shopping bags in the bathroom, then returns to the room. She sees the flowers on the bedside table, takes the card from the holder and reads it. LAURA gives a long strangled moan and slumps onto the bed sobbing, as KARLY comes through the connecting door, leaving it open.)

KARLY. Whatever is the matter? *(LAURA just wails louder, then continues sobbing and waves the note in the air. KARLY takes the note from her and reads:)* "For John and his new love" signed D.L.

(LAURA wails even louder.) That's nothing, read this.

(She hands her card to LAURA.)

> LAURA. *(Reading.)* "To my corporate love birds" signed D.L.
> KARLY. I'll kill him.
> LAURA. Who's this D.L.?
> KARLY. Never mind who D.L. is. We'd better find our husbands and nip this little weekend in the bud before it gets started. *(She goes into room 13.)* Let's see if we can find out where they are.

(She has crossed L. to the phone, she dials and the phone on the counter rings.)

> LAURA. *(By the connecting door.)* I can't believe they would do something like this. It's got to be that horrible D.L. person who's behind it all.

(Enter MRS. CARLSON from the office.)

> MRS. C. *(Picks up the counter phone.)* Reception.

(The phone in room 11 rings. LAURA crosses R. to answer it.)

> KARLY. This is Mrs. McGachen in room 13, do you happen to know where my husband is?

(The phone on the table rings.)

> MRS. C. Just a moment please. *(She pushes open the office door.)* Wilson could you get the other phone please?

(WILSON enters and crosses to the table phone.)

> LAURA. *(Picks up the phone in room 11.)* Hello.
> MRS. C. No you may not have it each way at five o'clock.
> WILSON. *(Has now picked up the table phone, but turns to MRS*

CARLSON.) If you want it each way you'd better talk to that guy in room 13.

KARLY. But I'm in room 13.

LAURA. *(Calling through the connecting door to KARLY.)* Do we know anything about a little green man?

MRS. C. What do you mean, do I think he'll need to whip it?

WILSON. I meant the guy who *was* in room 13.

KARLY. That's my husband you nit-wit.

LAURA. Who's a nit-wit?

MRS. C. I said whip it, not nit-wit, you idiot.

WILSON. Who are you calling an idiot?

KARLY. Who is this?

LAURA. I think I must be the nit-wit.

MRS. C. No, no, you idiot.

WILSON. I told you, don't call me an idiot.

MRS. C. For heaven's sake, who is this?

LAURA. If I'm not the nit-wit, then I suppose I must be the idiot.

MRS. C. *(Yelling.)* STOP! *(There is a stunned silence as she continues in a low calm voice.)* Now, I want everyone, in every room in this club to hang up their phone on the count of three. One—two—three. *(Everyone hangs up.)* Now Wilson, if you don't fix these phones, I am personally going to do you grievous bodily harm, and you can start by changing the phone in room 13. That seems to be the one causing all the trouble, and while you're at it, change the wire that goes into the jack.

(Exits to office.)

KARLY. *(Crosses into room 11, leaving the connecting door open.)* Come on, they've got to be somewhere.

(KARLY and LAURA exit room 11. WILSON goes behind the counter, picks up the phone, listens for a second then bends down behind the counter as KARLY and LAURA come D.)

LAURA. Do you suppose they were in it together?

KARLY. I don't know about together, but I'll tell you one thing, they are certainly in it now, and that D.L. person is definitely going to be made to pay.

(They exit to the front entrance.)

   WILSON. *(Stands up.)* Pay! It's worse than I thought. I don't believe it!

(Exits to office. Enter D.L., JOHN, DAVID and TINA from U.R. on the landing. D.L. is supporting JOHN. DAVID and TINA follow a step or two behind. They pause on the landing.)

   D.L. I'm so sorry you're not feeling well.
   JOHN. I think I just need to lie down a bit that's all.
   D.L. I'll help get you to bed.

(They head L. to room 13.)

   TINA. I told you something would go wrong.
   DAVID. Sh! we can still do it. Come on.

(They head L. on the landing. TINA goes into room 11. She sees the champagne, pours herself a glass, pulls down the covers a little, props up the pillows, and sits up on the bed sipping her champagne. Meanwhile, JOHN and D.L. have entered room 13, leaving the door ajar.)

   D.L. *(Pulling the covers back on the bed.)* Perhaps you'd like to slip your dress off.
   JOHN. *(A little too quickly.)* No. That is—er—I'm feeling quite faint. I think I'll just get right in.

(He takes off his shoes and gets into bed. DAVID has now entered room 13, leaving the door ajar.)

   DAVID. She'll be just fine now. Thank you, D.L.
   D.L. Good. I'll look in a little later. *(Notices TINA through the*

open connecting door, and goes into room 11.) I'm delighted to see you relaxing a bit Mrs. Baker. By the way, where's your husband?

(DAVID and JOHN react.)

 TINA. He's—er—er—*(DAVID, just on the room 13 side of the connecting door, is frantically signaling behind D.L.'s back and pointing to the bathroom.)*—he's in the bathroom.

(DAVID signals to JOHN, who gets the dress and wig off and stuffs them under the pillow. DAVID steps into room 11, puts his arm round D.L.'s shoulders, and walks her a step or two D.S., as JOHN, now in undershirt and boxer shorts, tip-toes behind them, over the bed and into the bathroom.)

 DAVID. You know D.L., I've noticed how very much you care about your staff. You seem to take a personal interest in every one of them. I'd be willing to bet that there's not much goes on behind your back that you're not aware of.
 D.L. Well I do pride myself in always knowing what's going on around me.

(JOHN, still in his shorts, now appears in the doorway of the bathroom. D.L. turns and sees him. JOHN gives a little cry, then leaps into the bed, R. side and pulls the covers up. TINA reacts to this by getting out of the bed L. side.)

 JOHN. Oh, excuse me D.L.
 D.L. No, please excuse me. *(She then turns to TINA, takes her by the arm and coaxes her back onto the bed.)* It's alright, there's nothing to be afraid of. Just have a little more champagne. *(TINA gets back into bed, carefully keeping her distance from JOHN.)* There, that's better. Now, I think we should all leave the two little honeymooners alone. I'll just check on Mrs. McGachen.
 DAVID. *(Moves quickly to block the connecting door, a look of panic on his face.)* I'm sure she's just fine D.L.

(At this point, JOHN is sitting up in the bed in room 11, R. side.
TINA, still with a glass of champagne in her hand, is sitting up in
the bed, L. side. DAVID blocks the connecting door with D.L.
immediately to his R. The following happens in a very rapid se-
quence:
1. *D.L. turns to face DAVID, her back now to JOHN and TINA.*
2. *JOHN reaches over, grabs the champagne glass from TINA, spills*
   the champagne all over the rear of D.L.'s skirt, and hands the
   glass back to TINA.
3. *As D.L. twists and bends down facing D.S. to look at her skirt,*
   JOHN leaps over TINA, moves L. behind D.L. and DAVID, leaps
   into the bed in room 13, puts on the wig and sits holding the cov-
   ers up to his neck.
4. *TINA leans over R. in the bed, as though embracing the unseen*
   figure of JOHN.
5. *DAVID follows JOHN into room 13, gets into the bed, R. side,*
   puts his arm round JOHN and smiles at D.L. who has followed
   him into room 13.

D.L. Excuse me, I just need to sponge my skirt.

(She crosses L. below the bed and exits to the bathroom. TINA gets
out of bed, closes the connecting door and exits to bathroom 11,
taking with her the champagne glass and bottle, as the door to
room 13 starts to open. DAVID still has his arm round JOHN in
the bed. KARLY and LAURA, having entered from the front door
now step into room 13.)

KARLY. David!
LAURA. John!

CURTAIN

ACT II

(The action is continuous.)

DAVID. Karly!
JOHN. Laura!
KARLY. David, what the hell is going on here?
LAURA. *(Starts to sob.)* Oh John!
DAVID. What are you doing here?
KARLY. I think I'll ask the questions David.
LAURA. *(Sobbing.)* Oh John!

WILSON has come out of the office, with a telephone in his hand, and gone up to room 13. He appears in the open doorway, gives a cursory knock and enters. He stops dead in his tracks, looks, first at the two figures in the bed, then at LAURA and KARLY.)

WILSON. I don't believe it! *(He shakes his head, rolls his eyes heavenward as JOHN and DAVID smile at him.)* I'm leaving, the phones can wait.

He exits room 13, leaving the door open, then goes R., comes D. and exits to the office.)

DAVID. You're supposed to be in Bloomingdales.
KARLY. Oh, you were counting on that weren't you. It's all very convenient isn't it. We go to Sax on Fifth Avenue, while you go for sex in room 13. I'll bet you two were just having a gay old time!
LAURA. *(Sobbing.)* Oh John!

JOHN. *(Gets out of bed, R. side. He takes off the wig and leaves it on the bed. He tries to take LAURA's hands in his, but she pulls away.)* Laura, please, it's not what you think. We can explain everything.

DAVID. *(Gets out of bed, L. side.)* There's no time for explanations. They've got to go. If D.L. finds our real wives, we're dead.

KARLY. D.L.? Real wives?

LAURA. Real wives?

JOHN. David's right, you've got to go. Wait in here, we'll explain everything in a minute.

(He hustles them into room 11. LAURA sits at the foot of the bed and starts to sob again. KARLY sits to her L. and puts an arm round her.)

KARLY. Now, now, come on.

JOHN. Please Laura. You see we met D.L. and then David said he wanted me to be his wife.

LAURA. *(Howling.)* Oh John!

DAVID. *(Now in the doorway, nervously glancing at the bathroom door in 13.)* You'd better get back in here, get that wig on and get into bed.

KARLY. That's disgusting.

LAURA. Oh John!

JOHN. He's right.

DAVID. Quickly.

(DAVID and JOHN return to room 13, closing the connecting door. JOHN gets the wig on and they get into bed, clutching the covers up to their chins, as before. DAVID R., JOHN L. They watch the bathroom door. Enter TINA from bathroom 11, closing the door. She has the bottle of champagne in one hand and the glass in the other. She is now obviously a little tipsy.)

TINA. Hi! You all come to join the party?

KARLY. Who are you? What are you doing here?

TINA. I seem to have lost my husband, and we're supposed to b on our honeymoon.

LAURA. *(Sobbing.)* Now there's another woman.

KARLY. What are you doing in this room? Wait a minute. Who s your husband?

TINA. Oh, he's real cute.

KARLY. What's his name?

TINA. John Baker.

LAURA. *(Howling.)* O-o-o-o-h!

KARLY. Laura, pull yourself together. We're going to get to the bottom of this. Now, *(She gets up, crosses R. and then backs TINA up against the bathroom door.)* you'd better come up with some answers.

TINA. I don't think so.

She runs L. over the bed to escape from KARLY, still carrying the champagne bottle and glass, exits room 11, then R. on the landing, then down to the front entrance, followed by KARLY and LAURA.)

KARLY. Come on Laura. Let's go. *(Now on the landing.)* Honymoon indeed! Just who do you think you are?

TINA. *(On the dead run.)* Don't get so mad, I'm his wife.

LAURA. No you're not, I'm his wife.

Exeunt running front entrance.

Enter MRS. CARLSON from the office, followed by WILSON, just in time to hear the last few words, but not in time to see TINA, who had just rounded the D.R. corner to the front entrance.)

MRS. C. That's it! They're wife swapping! That's all the proof I need. Wilson go and check who's in room 13, while I go and catch those two hussies.

Exits front entrance. WILSON mouths the word "hussies" to himself and makes his way up to room 13.)

JOHN. I don't think we should just be sitting here, what about Carly and Laura?

DAVID. We'd better sit tight for a couple of minutes till we can get rid of D.L. Then we'll be able to explain to our wives. Sh!

(Enter D.L. from the bathroom. She has left her jacket in the bathroom and is wearing a towel wrapped around her waist. She is carrying her skirt and slip, as WILSON appears in the doorway of room 13.)

D.L. Please excuse me, but I'm sure you understand how very much easier it was to get at everything once I'd taken my skirt off.

WILSON. *(Looks at JOHN and DAVID, then at D.L.)* I don't believe it!

(Exits R. on the landing and returns to the office.)

D.L. Mr. McGachen, what are you doing in bed?

DAVID. *(Hurriedly gets out of bed R. side.)* I—er—I just thought I'd comfort—er—my wife a little. How are you feeling now dear?

JOHN. Perhaps a little better, thank you—dear.

D.L. Good. Mr. McGachen, do you suppose you could leave us girls alone for a moment please?

DAVID. Sure.

JOHN. Please don't leave me alone.

D.L. You won't be alone. I'll be here.

JOHN. That's what I'm worried about.

D.L. What was that?

DAVID. She said it's time I went out. So, I'll leave you two alone then. I'll—er—I'll be on the terrace D.L.

(Exits 13 and R. to the terrace.)

D.L. I was just a little embarrassed to ask in front of your husband, but could you please go to my room and bring me a dry skirt and slip? You'll find a navy blue skirt and a white slip in the closet.

JOHN. Me?

D.L. Yes.

JOHN You want me to go and get them?

D.L. Well, I can hardly go myself looking like this. *(She removes the towel revealing underwear, etc. JOHN looks away in embarrass-ment.)* The door's open. You know, just to be on the safe side, I think I'll sponge this skirt one more time.

(Exits to bathroom 13. JOHN gets out of bed, still in his underwear, and, wearing the wig, takes a blanket off the bed, wraps it around himself, and exits room 13, closing the door. Enter WILSON from the office, just in time to see JOHN move furtively to the door of room 8.)

WILSON. Having a bad hair day are we sir?

(JOHN, realizes he is still wearing the wig, snatches it off, and goes quickly into room 8.)

WILSON. *(Raises his eyes heavenward.)* I don't believe it.

(Exits to office. TINA, still carrying the champagne bottle and glass, enters from the terrace. She looks behind her to see if anyone is following, then goes into room 11, closing the door. She pours herself another glass, puts down the bottle on the bedside table, takes the glass with her and exits to the bathroom, closing the door. She is followed from the terrace by MRS. CARLSON, who looks around and then goes into room 13, leaving the door open. JOHN enters from room 8, now carrying a skirt and slip. He heads to room 13. MRS. CARLSON hears him coming as she looks briefly out of the door of 13. She looks around for some-where to hide and finally dives under the bed as JOHN enters room 13, closing the door. He puts the blanket back on the bed, puts on the wig, knocks on the bathroom door and then dives for the bed, just managing to get under the covers as D.L. opens the bathroom door, and steps into the room.)

JOHN. *(Holding one arm out of the covers.)* I've got your things.
D.L. *(Takes the skirt and slip.)* Thank you.
JOHN. You're welcome.

D.L. Now that we're alone, I'd like your opinion on Mrs. Baker's little problem.

JOHN. Problem?

D.L. Yes, you do know why they're here this weekend?

(She disappears momentarily into the bathroom.)

JOHN. Sure, they're here to play golf.

D.L. *(Reappears in the bathroom doorway, without her towel. JOHN, acutely embarrassed, pulls the covers over his head, and doesn't hear D.L. say:)* They're on their honeymoon.

(She returns to the bathroom.)

JOHN. I still don't understand what the problem is.

D.L. *(Reappears in the bathroom doorway with her slip in her hand. John again covers his head.)* The problem is, it's their wedding night. *(She is about to step into the slip when she pauses and looks at JOHN.)* Am I embarrassing you like this?

JOHN. *(Peeks out.)* Perhaps a little.

D.L. Oh, just a second then.

(Goes back into the bathroom.)

JOHN. *(Almost to himself.)* What's the big deal about a game of golf?

D.L. *(Comes out of the bathroom fastening her skirt.)* What really worries me is that she says—er—she says—er—you know—she's never done it.

JOHN. Done it?

D.L. Yes.

JOHN. That's the problem?

D.L. No, in fact I find that rather refreshing these days. The problem is she told me she wasn't going to do it.

JOHN. So?

D.L. We need to help her.

JOHN. O.K. That sounds easy enough.

D.L. It does?

JOHN. Sure, we'll just get someone to teach her how to swing.

(MRS. CARLSON'S head appears at the foot of the bed, eyes bulging.)

D.L. Swing?

JOHN. Yes, that's the most important part.

D.L. Do you really think so?

JOHN. Well, that and having your feet in the correct position.

D.L. Feet?

JOHN. Of course, if you've got your feet in the right position when you first start, everything else just fits into place.

(MRS. CARLSON reacts.)

D.L. You seem to know an awful lot about this.

JOHN. Well, not really, but I did take lessons, years ago, from a very experienced Scotsman.

D.L. Lessons?

JOHN. Oh yes.

D.L. It sounds like a long process. I'm not sure we have that much time.

JOHN. Oh don't worry, I'll find time to fit it in, but first I'll have to get her interest aroused.

D.L. I see, but can you persuade Mrs. Baker to—er—you know, cooperate?

JOHN. I don't see why not. I'll even take her out and see that she gets some practice if you like.

(MRS. CARLSON reacts.)

D.L. I don't think it will be necessary to go quite that far. I think perhaps talking to her would be enough.

JOHN. Well alright, but I always think there's nothing like some hands on experience.

D.L. Really?

JOHN. Yes, one on one with an experienced professional is definitely the way to go. *(MRS. CARLSON reacts.)* Anyway, you leave it to me, I'll take care of it.

D.L. Well, O.K., thank you. Now, I think I'll leave you to rest a little bit. It's time I got back to the others on the terrace. You can always join us later if you feel up to it.

JOHN. Thank you.

D.L. Right, maybe later then.

(She reaches into the bathroom for her jacket, and, carrying the jacket and original skirt and slip, exits room 13, closing the door, then goes R. into room 8, closing the door. JOHN, still wearing the wig, hurries through the connecting door almost closing it. MRS. CARLSON climbs out from under the bed and comes just below the connecting door to listen. TINA enters room 11 from the bathroom, now minus shoes, blouse and skirt. She is wearing a pretty lace full slip, and carrying her glass.)

TINA. Let's have some more bubbly! *(She refills her now empty glass from the bottle on the bedside table.)* Why don't you have some *(Giggles.)* it'll put lead in your pencil!

JOHN. I wasn't planning on writing to anybody.

TINA. *(Obviously quite tipsy.)* Can we start our honeymoon now?

JOHN. *(Goes into bathroom 11.)* Now cut that out.

TINA. *(Strikes a sexy pose on the bed and sips her champagne.)* That's no way to speak to your new wife.

(MRS. CARLSON reacts, then creeps out of room 13, closing the door, and comes D. to the lobby.)

JOHN. *(In the doorway of bathroom 11, starts to put on his shirt and pants.)* Don't you start. I'm in enough trouble already.

TINA. *(Giggles.)* When you're on your honeymoon, aren't you supposed to take your pants off, not put them on?

JOHN. How much of that stuff have you had?

TINA. Just a iddy-biddy, teensy-weensy little bit.

JOHN. Oh my God! That's just what we need.

(All four phones ring simultaneously.)

TINA. *(Picks up the phone in room 11.)* Hello.

MRS. C. *(Now at the counter, picks up the phone.)* Oakfield Golf and Country Club.

WILSON. *(Enters from the office to answer the phone. MRS. CARLSON indicates he should pick up the phone on the table, which continues to ring. He crosses L. and picks it up.)* Yes?

JOHN. *(Now in his original shirt and pants, but still wearing the wig, has crossed L. into room 13 and picked up the phone.)* Hello.

TINA. *(Holds the phone, but giggles and calls through the connecting door.)* Why don't you take your pants off?

WILSON. *(Into the phone.)* What, right here in the lobby. I'll catch me' death of cold.

JOHN. No—no. Not you, I think she means me.

MRS. C. I don't care how good Golden Girl was last time in the final stretch, you may not put anything on anyone, anyhow, anytime, anywhere. Do I make myself clear?

WILSON. *(To MRS. CARLSON.)* Hold on a minute. Keep your pants on.

TINA. No—no. You need to take them off.

MRS. C. First you want me to put something on, now you want to take your pants off?

JOHN. It's alright, she means me.

MRS. C. Who's she? Who is this? What? What do you mean she's always at her best in a big field. That's disgusting.

WILSON. *(Directly to MRS. CARLSON.)* Take it easy Mrs. C. Keep your hair on.

TINA. And that's another thing. What are you doing with all that hair?

(JOHN snatches off the wig.)

MRS. C. What hair?

JOHN. I think she means my hair.

MRS. C. What?

JOHN. *(Calls to room 11.)* It's alright, I've taken it off.

MRS. C. I don't care what it is you've taken off young man, I strongly advise you to put it back on again.

(JOHN puts the wig back on.)

TINA. Don't put it on, take it off. *(JOHN takes the wig off.)* Let's take it all off.
MRS. C. Wilson, do something!
WILSON. What do you want me to do? I've told you, it's the wires under there.

(He points to the counter.)

TINA. Who's in their underwear?
JOHN. You are.
MRS. C. O-o-oh!
WILSON. Hang in there Mrs. C.
TINA. That's it, let's go and hang out somewhere.
JOHN. You're already hanging out.
MRS. C. Now everybody listen to me. We are not hanging in. We are certainly not hanging out. What we are doing is hanging up. NOW! *(They all hang up. JOHN goes briefly into the bathroom in room 13, as TINA, champagne glass in hand exits room 11, closing the door, wanders R. on the landing, and then comes D.)* Wilson, I don't care what you have to do, or how late you have to work, if you value your—(She pauses.) I was going to say "job", but I've changed my mind. If you value your life, *fix these phones.*

(Exits to office. WILSON crosses R., bends down behind the counter, then stands up briefly, his hands full of tangled wires.)

WILSON. "If you value your life—fix these phones." Oh sure.

(He disappears down behind the counter.)

JOHN. *(Returns to room 11.)* Now let's get dressed and—*(Doesn't see TINA.)* Tina, Tina. *(Looks in the bathroom.)* Oh no!

He rushes out of room 11 and R. on the landing. TINA has wandered D.S., the glass of champagne still in her hand, and is just to the R. of the couch as JOHN comes down the steps.)

JOHN. Oh good grief!
TINA. What's the matter Johnny-Poo?
JOHN. You can't walk around like that.
TINA. You're telling me?
JOHN. *(Realizes he is still wearing the wig and snatches it off, as TINA moves L., puts her glass down on the table, and strikes a sexy pose on the chair.)* What are you doing?
TINA. Waiting for you lover-boy.

She grabs him and tries to kiss him. Enter DAVID from the terrace.)

DAVID. What's going on?
JOHN. She's been drinking champagne all night.
DAVID. *(Looks around nervously and comes D.)* You'd better over her up. If D.L. sees her like that she'll have a heart attack.
JOHN. *(Comes L. behind the couch, puts the wig on the table, picks up the afghan, comes behind Tina on the chair, and tries to drape it over her. Tina tries to kiss him.)* Give me a hand will you.

DAVID comes D. below and L. of the chair as the counter phone rings.)

DAVID. John—quickly.

The following happens, almost simultaneously in a very rapid sequence:
. *DAVID drapes the afghan over TINA, covering her face but exposing her legs, which she crosses.*
. *JOHN crouches down behind the chair and leans forward, holding the afghan up to his chin, so the audience see TINA'S knees and lower legs but JOHN'S head, looking like one body. TINA'S right arm and JOHN'S left arm are visible. WILSON stands up to answer the phone.)*

WILSON. *(Looking curiously at JOHN/TINA.)* Golf Club. You want the boss? That'd be Mrs. Carlson, just a minute. *(He puts down the phone on the counter, pauses and looks at JOHN, who just smiles at him.)* Nice legs!

(TINA slowly and deliberately uncrosses her legs. WILSON raises his eyebrows to the heavens and exits to the office.)

DAVID. John—the wig!

(JOHN drops the afghan, picks up the wig and gets it on his head.)

TINA. *(Picks up her glass in her R. hand.)* I need a little drink.

(MRS. CARLSON enters from the office. JOHN crouches down as before, holding the afghan up to his chin. DAVID stands behind the chair a little to JOHN's L. and helps hold the afghan up to JOHN's chin. During the following telephone conversation, TINA crosses and uncrosses her legs several times, as JOHN, trying to look nonchalant, smiles at MRS. CARLSON. TINA's R. arm, holding the glass, is outside the afghan. She waves the glass around as JOHN follows it with movements of his head and eyes and once is obliged to take a sip when TINA holds it up to his lips.)

MRS. C. *(Picks up the phone.)* This is Mrs. Carlson. Yes, I suppose you could call me the boss. What can I do for you? I'm sorry about that, we've been having trouble with the phones all day. What? You want a daily double? Of course we can accommodate you, we have several doubles available. Legs how much? Legs Eleven and Smiling Boy? *(TINA's legs do a quick cross and uncross, as DAVID smiles at MRS. CARLSON.)* What price? Well, our standard double is eighty-five dollars.

(The table phone rings. DAVID and JOHN look at each other. MRS. CARLSON indicates they should answer it. TINA hands the glass from her R. hand to JOHN's L., then picks up the phone with her

R. hand and smoothly holds it up to JOHN's R. ear.)

JOHN. Hello. Just a moment please. *(TINA holds the phone out towards MRS. CARLSON.)* It's for you.

MRS. C. *(To JOHN.)* I'll be right with them.

JOHN. *(As TINA smoothly puts the phone back to his R. ear.)* She'll be right with you.

MRS. C. Now sir, when would you like this double? Tomorrow, very well, your name sir? *(She pauses and writes.)* And do you have a credit card number for me please? *(She writes. TINA's "other" L. arm appears from behind the afghan and scratches her leg. MRS. CARLSON looks curiously at this as JOHN and DAVID smile nonchalantly.)* Thank you, I've got that. What? You want it on Cool Hand Luke if Legs Eleven scratches? What is all this scratching about? *(TINA quickly puts her L. arm back under the afghan.)* What? Yes, you have your double for tomorrow. Thank you, good-bye. *(She hangs up the counter phone and crosses L. to take the phone from "JOHN". TINA is waving it about with her R. hand. Eventually MRS. CARLSON manages to grab it, as JOHN just smiles at her.)* Hello, what? No sir, I can assure you that Golden Girl did not show anybody anything. Good day. *(She slams down the phone, takes one last puzzled look at TINA's legs then turns and heads to the office yelling.)* Wilson!

(Exits to office.)

JOHN. *(Puts down the glass on the table and lowers the blanket.)* Now what?

DAVID. We've got to get her out of here.

TINA. *(Tries to grab JOHN.)* Hello.

JOHN. If I take her out of here dressed like this she'll get arrested.

DAVID. I wouldn't worry about that if I were you, they'll arrest you first.

JOHN. *(Realizing he is still wearing the wig, takes it off and puts it on the back of the couch.)* Come on, let's get her moving.

(They get TINA on her feet, in front of the chair. DAVID is just to her

L. and JOHN still behind the chair. DAVID moves her R. just in front of the couch. JOHN reaches over the back of the couch trying to cover her with the afghan. TINA tries to grab him and she falls on the couch pulling JOHN on top of her.)

MRS. C. *(Enters from the office, stops in the half open door and turns back to talk to WILSON.)* I have to go out for a few minutes, so please stay here Wilson, and for heaven's sake, fix these phone.

(DAVID hastily arranges the afghan over JOHN and TINA. We see JOHN's head R. and TINA's feet L., about seven feet from end to end. MRS. CARLSON stops dead in her tracks, and moves slowly down to look at the figure under the afghan. JOHN and DAVID smile at her. She raises her eyebrows to the heavens and exits to the front entrance, as TINA waves goodbye with a foot.)

DAVID. Quickly.

(He gets the afghan off them. TINA picks up the glass and JOHN and TINA head U.S. to the landing as DAVID straightens the afghan on the back of the couch. Enter WILSON from the office.)

WILSON. *(To himself.)* Fix these phones! Ah, Mr. McGachen could you give me a hand?
DAVID. *(Looks U.S. as JOHN and TINA head to the landing.)* Well—I—er—
WILSON. It'll only take a minute.
DAVID. Well, O.K. What is it you need me to do?
WILSON. I've got to get into this junction box here. *(He indicates below the counter.)* Could you go in the office and pick up the phone if I can get it to ring.
DAVID. Sure.

(Exits to office.)

WILSON. *(Crouches down.)* Now let's see, it should be the red wire.

(JOHN and TINA enter room 11, she flings herself on the bed as JOHN closes the door. She puts her glass down and strikes a sexy pose.)

TINA. It's honeymoon time.

JOHN. Where are your clothes? *(Looks in the bathroom.)* Ah, *(He turns back to the bed and gets her up.)* Come on, let's get moving. I need you to get dressed.

TINA. *(Now out of sight in the bathroom.)* I don't want my clothes I want a drink.

JOHN. You can have a drink when you get your clothes on. Now get dressed, I'll be right back.

(He crosses L. through the connecting door and exits to the bathroom in room 13. TINA immediately reappears, she has removed her slip. She is now seen to be wearing a bra and tap pants. She giggles, pours herself another glass of champagne and gets into bed pulling the covers right over her head. There is some frantic giggling and wriggling under the covers, as first the bra, and then the pants, are thrown out of the bed. She then lies still.)

WILSON. *(Stands up and holds the office door open.)* Thanks Mr. McGachen, that was a big help.

DAVID. *(Enters from the office.)* You're welcome.

(He heads U.S. as WILSON bends down behind the counter again.)

D.L. *(Enters from Room 8, dressed as before but without the jacket she was carrying.)* Ah, Mr. McGachen, just the person I was looking for. I need to have a word with you. Do you have a minute?

DAVID. Certainly D.L.

(JOHN comes out of the bathroom of 13, crosses R., looks into room 11, looks in the bathroom, doesn't see TINA under the covers, exits room 11, then R. on the landing.)

D.L. Let's sit down for a moment.

DAVID. Of course.

(They sit, DAVID L. in the chair and D.L. to his R. on the couch.)

D.L. I really need to find your wife, it's very important that I talk to her. *(JOHN, who has now appeared on the landing, over-hears this and rushes back to room 13. He gets the dress out of the bed, picks up the shoes and goes into bathroom 13.)* You see, I've been having second thoughts about her helping Mrs. Baker with her little problem.
DAVID. Problem?
D.L. Yes, you remember, her reluctance to er - your know.
DAVID. Oh yes. That problem.
D.L. We've just had a conversation that really makes me wonder whether she's the right person for the job.
DAVID. I see, I think.
D.L. Yes, your wife said something that really made me wonder if they need professional help. I mean it's all very well having your feet in the right position so your hips move properly, but is that enough?
DAVID. *(Dumbstruck.)* What?

(JOHN, now in the dress and shoes, runs out of the bathroom, goes R. on the landing, and comes D. During the following conversation, seen by DAVID but not by D.L., he creeps D.S. signaling to DAVID that he needs the wig. He drops down behind the couch and tries to take the wig off the back of the couch. D.L. appears to notice it moving a couple of times and stops to look at it before continuing her conversation with DAVID.)

D.L. I suppose the fact that she had lessons counts for something.
DAVID. Lessons?
D.L. Yes.
DAVID. Is that what he—she said?
D.L. Oh yes.

(WILSON puts his head up over the counter and mouths the words as

DAVID says them:)

DAVID. I don't believe it.

(WILSON exits to the office.)

D.L. She must have had her training from the Scotsman before you were married, anyway, I think we ought to talk to her. Is she still lying down?

DAVID. *(Gets up and moves R.U.S. so as to shield the back of the couch from D.L. who comes U.R. to his L.)* Perhaps we should check the terrace D.L.

D.L. O.K. if you think so.

(DAVID and D.L. exit R. to the terrace. JOHN grabs the wig, rushes up to 13, closes the door behind him, makes sure the connecting door is closed, puts on the wig, and gets into bed pulling up the covers. DAVID and D.L. re-appear from the terrace and head L. to 13.)

DAVID. *(Looks D.S. and sees JOHN and the wig are now gone.)* I guess you were right D.L. I'll bet she's still lying down. *(He opens the door of 13 and sees the figure in the bed. He steps aside to allow D.L. to enter first, then follows her in.)* Are you asleep dear?

JOHN. *(Sits up.)* No dear.

D.L. Good, you see I've decided your approach to Mrs. Baker might just be a little too direct. We need a more subtle touch. Let's go and talk to them ourselves.

(She heads out of 13.)

DAVID. *(Pointing to room 11.)* Have a nice rest dear.

(He follows D.L. out and closes the door. JOHN leaps out of bed, opens the connecting door and goes into 11 closing the door behind him. He gets quickly into bed, takes off the wig and hides it under the pillow on the R. side of the bed as D.L. knocks on the door of room. 11.)

JOHN. Come in.

(D.L. enters with DAVID behind her.)

D.L. Please forgive the intrusion. *(Sees TINA's figure under the covers.)* It really looks as though everything has worked out after all. How is Mrs. Baker, John?

JOHN. Mrs. Baker? *(He sees them looking at TINA's figure and notices her for the first time.)* Oh. *(He lifts the covers a little and looks under. He sits up with a jolt, his eyes as big as saucers.)* Magnificent!

D.L. Really? Well, that's good, and we were so worried. You must think we're a couple of real boobs.

JOHN. Real boobs? *(Looks under the covers again.)* Yes.

D.L. What?

DAVID. He means no, don't you John?

JOHN. Yes, I mean no, that is yes.

D.L. You seem very distracted John, is something bothering you?

DAVID. I'm sure he's got one or two things on his mind, D.L.

JOHN. Yes, that's it. *(He looks under the covers again.)* As a matter of fact there are a couple of things.

DAVID. D.L. They are, after all, on their honeymoon, don't you think we ought to—er—?

D.L. You're absolutely right. Let's have that drink on the terrace Goodnight Mr. Baker.

JOHN. Goodnight, D.L.

D.L. *(Stops by the door of room 8.)* Why don't you go on ahead I'll be there in a minute.

(Exits room 8. DAVID exits to the terrace.)

JOHN. *(Takes a blanket off the bed, and, facing D.S., holds it out with both hands as TINA moves from the bed to the bathroom unseen by the audience.)* Tina, please get dressed. I'm going to take you home.

TINA. *(Reaches round the bathroom door and takes the glass of the bedside table.)* But I haven't finished the champagne.

JOHN. Just get dressed please. It's over. D.L. won't need to see you again.

TINA. *(Off.)* You're not taking me home dressed like that. I'd never hear the end of it.

JOHN. Right, you get dressed, I'll go and change.

(Exits to bathroom 13. Enter KARLY and LAURA from the front entrance.)

KARLY. She can't have gone far.

LAURA. Oh Karly, I just want to go home.

(She flops onto the sofa.)

KARLY. *(Crosses L. and sits in the chair.)* Not till we find out just exactly what those two no-good husbands of ours are up to.

(TINA has come out of bathroom 11, wrapped in a towel and dialed the phone. The counter phone rings and WILSON enters from the office to answer it.)

WILSON. Front desk.

TINA. This is room 11, I'd like another bottle of champagne please.

WILSON. Who is this?

TINA. *(Giggles.)* This is Mrs. Baker.

WILSON. Oh I see. Alright Mrs. Baker, one bottle of champagne coming right up.

TINA. Thank you Wilson.

(She hangs up and returns to bathroom 11. WILSON hangs up.)

LAURA. Karly, it's her.

KARLY. *(On her feet.)* Excuse me, but did I hear you say Mrs. Baker?

WILSON. That's right.

KARLY. Do you mind telling me which room she's in?

WILSON. Do you mind telling me who you are?

KARLY. You know who I am, you carried our bags in. I'm Mrs. McGachen.

WILSON. *(Beaming from ear to ear.)* That's right, and who's this?

(He indicates LAURA.)

KARLY. This is—*(She pauses, realizing the trap WILSON has set for her.)* Ah, yes, this is *(She pauses.)* Missy Baker.

WILSON. Missy Baker? I thought you said she was Mrs. Baker.

KARLY. Oh no, you must have been mistaken. This is Missy *(Pauses.)* Mrs. Baker's sister.

(LAURA smiles and gives WILSON a little finger wave.)

WILSON. I see. Well, the Bakers are in room 11, but I wouldn' go in there if I were you.

KARLY. Oh, and why not?

WILSON. Well, you know.

LAURA. *(Starts to bawl.)* O-o-o-h!

WILSON. What's wrong with her?

KARLY. Don't take any notice, she does this all the time.

(LAURA continues to sob.)

WILSON. *(Crosses L. and produces a large white handkerchie which he hands to LAURA.)* Here you are miss.

LAURA. *(Takes the handkerchief.)* Thank you. *(She makes a huge raspberry in it, wipes her nose and hands it back to WILSON.)* Thank you.

WILSON. *(Looks at the handkerchief.)* Why don't you keep it.

(He moves R. behind the counter.)

KARLY. *(Crosses R. to the counter.)* I've got it. Wilson, did hear you say Mrs. Baker, in room 11, wanted some champagne?

WILSON. That's right.

KARLY. How would you like—er—Missy here to deliver it. It'll be such a nice surprise for them.

WILSON. You're really into surprises aren't you? But I've got to get it from the stock room, and Mrs. Carlson is out, and I can't leave these phones.

KARLY. Oh! *(Pause.)* How long would it take you to get a bottle?

WILSON. About one minute I guess.

KARLY. Well, suppose we stay here and answer the phones?

WILSON. Well, I dunno—*(KARLY has produced a twenty dollar bill from her purse and is waving it in front of Wilson.)* What a good idea.

(He snatches the bill and exits to the front entrance.)

LAURA. What are you going to do?

KARLY. You'll see. (*The counter phone rings.*) Damn! I knew it. Oh dear. *(The phone rings again, she picks it up.)* Hello. *(She listens.)* What? *(Pauses.)* I'm afraid I don't understand. I'm just filling in for a moment. Could you call back in a few minutes? Thank you. *(Hangs up the phone.)* That's odd.

LAURA. What is?

KARLY. Well, someone on the other end of the phone said there's going to be a lot of action on number eleven, and they wanted to take everything off at six o'clock.

LAURA. *(Howling again.)* O-o-o-o-h!

(Enter WILSON from the front entrance, with a bottle of champagne in his hand.)

KARLY. *(Takes the champagne.)* Thank you Wilson. Come along Laura—I mean Missy.

They head up to the landing. WILSON shrugs and exits to the office. TINA, now dressed, enters from bathroom 11, crosses L. through the connecting door, closing it behind her. KARLY and Laura enter room 11, they cross R. to look in the bathroom. KARLY puts the champagne down on the bedside table. JOHN, now dressed in his original clothes, enters from bathroom 13.)

JOHN. O.K. Let's get going.

(He takes TINA's elbow, and propels her out of room 13, closing the door. They head R. on the landing.)

KARLY. That's funny. She's not here. Come on, you check the terrace, I'll check the pro-shop.

(They exit room 11, leaving the door open. KARLY heads L., LAURA R.)

TINA. *(As she appears with JOHN on the landing.)* But I don't want to go home, *(Giggles.)* let's play golf.
JOHN. I've told you, you're in no condition to drive. Now where's your car?

(They come down to the lobby, as LAURA reappears on the landing. She stops to listen.)

TINA. Why can't we start our honeymoon?
JOHN. Come on. You need to get home and into bed.
TINA. Oh Mr. Baker, what a lovely idea.

(They both exit, front entrance. LAURA breaks into loud sobbing comes D. and slumps into the chair with her head in her hands Enter D.L. from room 8, dressed as before. She sees LAURA and comes D. to sit to her R. on the couch.)

D.L. Is something wrong? *(LAURA makes more noise and blows a huge raspberry into her handkerchief.)* Whatever is the matter? *(Howls from LAURA.)* Nothing can be that bad. My name is Dorothy Can I help?
LAURA How would you like it if your husband was going on his

honeymoon with another woman?

D.L. What?

LAURA He's taking her home to bed.

D.L. Do you know who she is?

LAURA. No but she's probably got his fingerprints all over her.

D.L. You mean your husband—?

LAURA *(Howling again.)* Y-e-e-s!

D.L. Who is he? What's his name?

LAURA. John Baker.

D.L. What?

LAURA John Baker.

D.L. Your husband?

LAURA. Yes.

D.L. But you can't be his wife.

LAURA. And why not?

D.L. Because I've met his wife, and you're not her.

LAURA. That's what I mean.

D.L. Wait a minute. What's your name?

LAURA. Laura.

D.L. But you died.

LAURA. I did?

D.L. Yes, you were bitten by a tsetse fly.

LAURA. In Connecticut?

D.L. You were on vacation in Costa Rica.

LAURA. I was?

D.L. You survived.

LAURA. I did?

D.L. This is amazing. Does your husband know you're here?

LAURA. Yes, but he won't have anything to do with me. He says he's on his honeymoon.

D.L. Oh my God, that's right. We've got to stop it.

LAURA. Stop what?

D.L. The honeymoon of course. Do you know where they are?

LAURA. They just went out the front entrance.

D.L. Right, you stay here. I'll try and find them.

D.L. exits front entrance. LAURA continues to sob. Enter WILSON from the office.)

WILSON. You alright miss?
LAURA. I guess so.
WILSON. Right I'll get that new phone for 13 then.

(Exits to office. Enter KARLY from L. on the landing.)

KARLY. Oh, there you are. *(She comes D. and sits on the sofa.)* Listen, I just had a brilliant idea. Instead of chasing our no-good husbands all night, I thought of a much better way.
LAURA. What do you mean?
KARLY. We're going to get our revenge.
LAURA. How?
KARLY. We're going to find ourselves a couple of guys, preten they're our lovers, and see how those two Casanovas like a taste o their own medicine.
LAURA. But I don't want a lover, I just want John.
KARLY. Don't be silly, we're not actually going to do anything we're just going to make David and John jealous.
LAURA. Oh Karly, I don't think I'd be any good at that.
KARLY. Of course you will. Believe me, it'll work.
LAURA. Where are we going to find two guys? You heard wha the manager said, there's only that horrible D.L. Hutchison guy in th whole place.
KARLY. Well he can be one. *(She pauses thinking.)* There's go to be another man somewhere.

(Enter WILSON from the office with a phone and lead in his hand LAURA and KARLY, their mouths open, look at each other. WIL SON nods affably to them and goes up to room 13.)

LAURA. Not him.
KARLY. Why not?
LAURA. I don't think I could.
KARLY. Of course you could.
LAURA. Oh Karly, I wouldn't know what to do.

KARLY. Alright, I'll do it. *(Gets up.)* Follow me. *(They both head U.S. to the landing.)* Just watch and see how it's done. *(She stops.)* No, better still, find my husband *(She points R. to the terrace.)* and send him to room 13. *(LAURA exits R. to the terrace. KARLY heads to room 13. In the meantime, WILSON has entered room 13 and looked at the phone L. of the bed. He sees the lead going behind the headboard. He puts the new phone down, goes R. of the bed, un-plugs the wire and climbs over the bed removing it from behind the headboard. He then takes the new wire behind the headboard to the R. side of the bed. He is on his knees plugging in the new phone as KARLY enters. She closes the door and strikes a sexy pose against it.)* Hello Wilson.

WILSON. *(Struggling to get to his feet.)* Oh hello.

KARLY. Here, let me help you up. *(She faces him and pulls him up slowly. His head, first almost touching her stomach, then her chest until finally he is upright, his lips about one inch from hers.)* Has any-one ever told you, you're a very attractive man?

WILSON. *(Looks around to see who she is talking to.)* Me?

KARLY. Oh yes. I felt this spark between us, the very first time I set eyes on you.

WILSON. Me?

KARLY. Yes, you! Kiss me Wilson!

(As she lunges forward, WILSON falls backwards on to the bed. KARLY straddles him and tries to kiss him. WILSON struggles feebly. Enter MRS. CARLSON from the front entrance. She looks in the office.)

MRS. C. Wilson.

(She then heads U.S. and L. on the landing. WILSON pushes KARLY to one side, escapes over the foot of the bed and backs into room 11.)

WILSON. I don't believe it!

KARLY. Believe it.

WILSON. It must be contagious. Why me?

KARLY. Ever since I first saw you, with your bulging muscles carrying those suitcases, I knew I wanted you.

WILSON. Bulging muscles?

(KARLY, now just inside room 11, has WILSON backed up against the bed. As MRS. CARLSON starts to open the door of room 13, KARLY looks over her shoulder and sees it. She then pushes WILSON down on the bed, and straddles him again.)

KARLY. *(In a dramatic tone, for the benefit of the listener in room 13.)* You see my husband no longer excites me. *(MRS. CARLSON reacts.)* I need a real man, one like you. Oh yes, I know my husband has his playthings, but I'm not just going to play with you. We can share real passion together.

(DAVID and LAURA have entered from the terrace and crossed L. to Room 13. The following happens almost simultaneously, in a very rapid sequence. DAVID enters room 13 and bumps into MRS. CARLSON, who is standing with her back to the door trying to look into room 11. They clutch each other, stagger and fall on the bed in room 13. LAURA stops in the doorway of room 13. KARLY, who has been straddling WILSON now tries to embrace him. WILSON again escapes by rolling over towards the foot of the bed, as KARLY falls forward. WILSON stands up and goes to the connecting door. He sees DAVID and MRS. CARLSON in a very compromising position on the bed in room 13.)

WILSON. I don't believe it! Well, well, Mrs. Carlson, I see even you are joining in now.

MRS. C. *(Extricating herself and standing up.)* What?

WILSON. I'm beginning to see you in a whole new light.

MRS. C. Don't be ridiculous Wilson. What are you doing here anyway?

WILSON. I came to change the phone.

MRS. C. Well, does it work?

WILSON. I dunno. You told me to change it, not test it.

MRS. C. Alright, we'll test it later. Was that you in there Wilson?

WILSON. Me?

MRS. C. Do you see anyone else in here called Wilson?

WILSON. Now listen Mrs. C. I wasn't doing anything. It was all
her.

MRS. C. What do you mean "it was all her"?

WILSON. Well, when she saw me, she seemed to get excited.

MRS. C. What?

WILSON. Excited. You know, you remember "excited".

MRS. C. Well you must have shown her some encouragement.

WILSON. I've never showed her anything.

MRS. C. Alright, alright, I believe you. Now hurry up and see
what you can do about the office phones.

WILSON. Under normal circumstances Mrs. C., I'd be glad to
hurry up, *(He is eyeing KARLY warily as he moves past her.)* but I
seem to have developed this tendinitis, it runs right up my—

MRS. C. Wilson!

WILSON. Alright, alright, I'm going.

(Exits room 11, comes D. and into the office.)

MRS. C. There definitely something of an unsavory nature going
on in this club. I can't quite put my finger on it yet, but I will. I want
you to know I will not rest until I have determined who is responsible
and expelled them from the premises.

(Exits room 13, comes D. and into the office.)

LAURA. *(Still in the doorway of room 13.)* Oh Karly, what are
we going to do now?

KARLY. *(Now in the connecting doorway.)* Leave it to me.

DAVID. *(Has got off the bed, L. side.)* Karly, what on earth is
going on here?

KARLY. You're asking me?

LAURA. Can't we just go home?

DAVID. What were you doing in there with Wilson?

KARLY. *(Aside to LAURA.)* There, you see, I knew it would
work.

DAVID. What was that?

KARLY. I said you blew it you jerk.

DAVID. I can explain—

KARLY. I'm not sure I'm talking to you David. In any event. Laura and I have plans for this evening, so if you'll excuse us—

(KARLY and LAURA exit R. on the landing, come D. and exit to the front entrance.)

DAVID. *(Following them.)* What do you mean you have plans for this evening? Karly please, I can explain everything, it's not at al what you think. Karly!

(Enter MRS. CARLSON from the office. LAURA and KARLY have jus rounded the corner to the front entrance and DAVID is abou level with the office door.)

MRS. C. Ah, Mr. McGachen, could I have a word with you please?

DAVID. Well, I—er—*(He looks after KARLY and LAURA wanting to follow them, then gives up.)* Oh, I suppose so.

MRS. C. *(Indicates the couch with her L. hand.)* Let's sit down for a moment.

(DAVID comes D.L. to the front of the couch. MRS. CARLSON is now just to his R. her back almost to the front entrance. Enter TIN. from the front entrance, on the dead run, looking behind her. She crashes into MRS. CARLSON from behind, who falls into DAVID, who falls backwards on the couch with MRS. CARLSON on top of him. TINA continues on into room 11, closes the door notices the new bottle of champagne, picks it up with a glass and exits to the bathroom closing the door. WILSON enters from the office.)

WILSON. I don't believe it! You really ought to control yoursel Mrs. C. There are bedrooms for this sort of thing you know.

MRS. C. *(Stands up and straightens her clothing.)* What on earth are you talking about?

WILSON. There's life in the old girl yet eh?

MRS. C. What?

WILSON. I've figured out what's going on with you and Mr. McGachen. I'm not stupid you know.

MRS. C. If your I.Q. was one point higher you could be a basket-ball!

DAVID. *(Now on his feet.)* She's quite right, we just had a little accident.

WILSON. Sure!

MRS. C. Wilson, that's enough. Would you now please go to room 13 and call the desk. Let's see if at least one phone is working.

(WILSON goes up to room 13. Enter LAURA and D.L. from the front entrance.)

D.L. Ah, Mrs. Carlson, you haven't seen Mr. Baker have you?

MRS. C. I saw him a little earlier, stretching his legs with Mr. McGachen.

D.L. I see. Well if you see him would you please tell him we'd like to see him in his room.

MRS. C. You and Mrs. Baker?

D.L. Yes.

MRS. C. You're both going to his room are you?

D.L. Yes. It's very important that we get together with him.

MRS. C. Both of you?

D.L. Well, yes.

MRS. C. At the same time?

D.L. Yes.

MRS. C. Let me get this straight. You and Mrs. Baker want to get together in the same room with Mr. Baker?

D.L. Yes.

MRS. C. And what do *you* think about that Mrs. Baker?

LAURA. I think it's wonderful that Dorothy has offered to help us.

MRS. C. That's disgusting.

DAVID. I can assure you Mrs. Carlson that—

MRS. C. *(To DAVID.)* Mr. McGachen, please don't tell me that you're going to join this sordid assignation?

DAVID. Well actually I thought I'd just go and check on Mrs. McGachen.

D.L. No, Mr. McGachen. I'd like you to come to room 11 with us please. There's something we all have to do together urgently.

(MRS. CARLSON reacts and raises her eyes heavenward as she turns to go into the office. Meanwhile WILSON has entered room 13 and dialed the phone. The counter phone rings.)

MRS. C. *(Picks up the counter phone.)* Oakfield Golf and Country Club.

(The table phone rings. MRS. CARLSON gestures to LAURA to answer it, which she does.)

LAURA. Hello.

WILSON. Hello.

MRS. C. Is that you Wilson?

WILSON. Yes ma-am.

MRS. C. Excellent, we've solved one problem then.

LAURA. Excuse me, but there's a man on the phone who wants to know how much it will cost him to lay Singing Mistress. What? *(She listens to the phone again.)* Oh, I see. He says he wants to lay on Singing Mistress. What? *(Listens again.)* Lay off on Singing Mistress?

WILSON. I'll be right down Mrs. C.

(Hangs up, exits room 13 closing the door, and heads R. on the landing.)

MRS. C. *(Hangs up her own phone, strides L. and takes the phone from LAURA.)* Who is this? I see. Well I want you to know there will be no laying either on or off anyone's Singing Mistress. There are no singing mistresses here. Listen! *(She holds the phone at arm's length and moves it around in all directions.)* Do you hear any mistresses singing? What? I've just told you there are no mistresses here, and if there were, let me assure you, that in keeping with the

reputation and high level of respectability, for which this club is well
known—hello? *(Looks around then hangs up.)*—They hung up.

WILSON. *(Who has come D. to the counter.)* So would I if I got
that earful.

MRS. C. What did you say?

WILSON. I said "so could I but I'm not that cheerful".

D.L. Come on everyone, we must find Mr. Baker.

(D.L., LAURA and DAVID go up to the landing and head L.)

MRS. C. *(Heads for the office.)* Come along Wilson, let's get
moving.

(Exits to office.)

WILSON. *(Following her.)* I'd be able to go a lot faster if it was-
n't for this chronic hip joint of mine. You see —

*(Exits to office, muttering to himself.
D.L. knocks and enters room 11, followed by LAURA and DAVID.)*

D.L. We simply must find the honeymooners. *(Looks through the
open connecting door.)* Oh look, Mrs. McGachen's up. She must be
feeling better. I wonder where she went.

DAVID. She probably went back to the terrace. I'll go and see.

D.L. Well I really did want to talk to you about Mrs. Baker, but that
can wait a few minutes I suppose. Tell you what, why don't we all go?

DAVID. No! I'll go. *(He rushes out of room 11 and runs R. out
to the terrace.)*

D.L. Goodness, what's his hurry?

LAURA. Can we please find my husband?

D.L. Of course, come along.

(They exit room 11, closing the door, and go R. on the landing.)

LAURA. Thank you.

D.L. *(Now by the door of room 8.)* Come in for a second, I really need to get my jacket.

(D.L. and LAURA exit to room 8. Enter TINA from bathroom 11, carrying the champagne bottle and glass. She is now obviously very tipsy. She has once again removed her shoes, jacket and skirt and is again seen in the lace slip. She pours yet another glass of champagne, drinks, puts the glass and bottle down on the bedside table, yawns, then gets into bed pulling the covers right up over her head.
Enter DAVID in a hurry from the terrace. He comes D. towards the front entrance, as MRS. CARLSON enters from the office.)

MRS. C. Ah, Mr. McGachen.

DAVID. *(Stops L. of the counter.)* Yes?

MRS. C. *(Looks around to make sure they are alone.)* Mr McGachen. I realize of course that in this particular instance it is Mr Baker, and not yourself who seems to be the object of the desires of those two *(She raises her eyes to the heavens.)* promiscuous philanderers, but I do hope that you are not a party to any of these lascivious undertakings.

DAVID. Promiscuous philanderers, lascivious undertakings?

MRS. C. Yes indeed, and when you see Mr. Baker— *(JOHN appears from the front entrance, seen by DAVID but not by MRS. CARLSON. DAVID raises both hands in front of him, palms facing away thumbs about six inches apart, to signal to JOHN to stop and go back out. JOHN backs quickly out of sight.)* —you might tell him—

(She trails off looking at DAVID.)

DAVID. *(Quickly puts his thumbs together, as though framing a camera shot.)* Yes, that would be perfect for our next TV commercial. You behind the counter. I can see it now, "What Ashley Maureen make-up can do for the busy executive". A whole series entitled "Beauty in Club Management". You would be perfect.

(He moves around a little, framing other shots of MRS. CARLSON with his hands.)

MRS. C. *(A little flustered.)* Oh my, do you think so?

DAVID. Just magnificent, such grace, such beauty.

MRS. C. Oh my goodness, do you really mean that?

DAVID. Absolutely. *(MRS. CARLSON poses by the desk. DAVID frames her with his hands and "snaps" a photo. Mrs. Carlson, really carried away now, pulls some pins out of her hair which cascades down. She goes to the desk and strikes several "pin-up" poses on one leg. DAVID is obliged to keep "snapping". Finally he lowers his hands.)* Now, you were saying?

MRS. C. *(Fluffs her hair.)* Oh nothing, nothing at all.

(Makes a dramatic turn, shakes her hair and exits to the office.)

DAVID. Oh God! *(Runs D.R.)* John. John.

JOHN. *(Enters D.R.)* What was all that about?

DAVID. Believe me, you didn't want to run into Mrs. Carlson. Listen, D.L. found out you weren't in bed— *(He hears the door of room 8 start to open, and pushing JOHN down, he ducks below the counter, as D.L. and LAURA enter from room 8, and exit R. to the terrace. They stand up.)* She's gone looking for you now. What were you doing?

JOHN. Well, Tina's been drinking champagne all night, and I tried to get her into her car to take her home, but she ran away from me.

DAVID. *(Hustling him U.S.)* Come on. You've got to get back in bed in room 13. You've got to be my wife, one more time.

(They exit U.L. on the landing as MRS. CARLSON, who has obviously been listening, creeps out of the office.)

MRS. C. Ah-ha!

(She follows them U.S. then L. on the landing. Enter WILSON from the office who follows MRS. CARLSON. JOHN and DAVID enter room 13, leaving the door open.)

DAVID. O.K. Now, where's the wig and dress?

JOHN. The dress is right here, the wig's in the other room. I'll get it.

(He crosses R. into room 11, leaving the connecting door open, goes to the R. side of the bed, and takes the wig out from under the pillows.)

DAVID. We'll just let D.L. see you back in bed, tell her you went to the bathroom or something, and then we'll call it a night. We'll get rid of her, find the girls and explain everything. Now let's get you into—

(MRS. CARLSON has entered room 13. DAVID, who is standing in the connecting doorway, talking to JOHN in room 11, turns and bumps into MRS. CARLSON, who falls backwards onto the bed, pulling DAVID on top of her, as WILSON enters room 13. JOHN immediately throws the dress behind him into the bathroom 11, leaps over TINA, puts on the wig and sits up on the L. side holding the covers up to his neck.)

WILSON. *(In the doorway of room 13, looking at MRS. CARLSON and DAVID.)* I don't believe it! Still, I did say there were beds for this sort of thing.
DAVID. *(Gets up.)* Mrs. Carlson. I really am so very sorry, I didn't see you come in.
MRS. C. *(Gets off the bed, very flustered.)* That's alright. I'm beginning to get quite used to it.
WILSON. I didn't think you had it in you Mrs. C.
MRS. C. Don't look so surprised Wilson. I'll have you know Mr McGachen wants to use me in a beauty commercial.
WILSON. You?
MRS. C. Certainly. You know I think I'll go on a diet. I could lose five pounds a week.
WILSON. Good. By Christmas you'll be gone altogether.
MRS. C. Wilson! *(She tries to look into room 11, where JOHN sitting up in bed, has turned away R. so all MRS. CARLSON can see is the back of his head.)* Is that Mrs. McGachen?
DAVID. Yes, we were just going to bed. *(Goes into 11, sits on*

the bed and puts his arm round JOHN's shoulders.) Weren't we my
little pumpkin?

JOHN. *(Still facing R.)* What? *(DAVID digs an elbow into him.)*
Oh yes.

DAVID. Say goodnight to Mrs. Carlson.

JOHN. Goodnight Mrs. Carlson.

MRS. C. *(Still peering into room 11, trying to see John's face.)*
Goodnight Mrs. McGachen. Come along Wilson.

*(She exits room 13, past WILSON, then R. on the landing and D. to
the office. WILSON pauses for a moment and looks into room 11,
JOHN turns, both he and DAVID smile at him and give him a
little finger wave.)*

WILSON. I don't believe it!

*(He exits room 13, closing the door, and follows MRS. CARLSON R.
on the landing and D. to the office.)*

DAVID. *(Stands up.)* Right, into the other bed.

JOHN. Yes my little pumpkin!

DAVID. Sorry about that.

JOHN. David!

(He points to the lump on the R. side of the bed.)

DAVID. *(Whispers.)* Who?

JOHN. I haven't a clue.

DAVID. *(There is a slight pause as they look at each other.)*
Don't you think we ought to find out?

JOHN. *(Gingerly pulls back the covers.)* It's Tina. *(He manages
to get her a little more upright on the pillows.)* She's passed out.

*(D.L. and LAURA have entered from the terrace and crossed L. to
room 13. As they open the door, DAVID grabs the wig off
JOHN'S head and leaps into the L. side of the bed totally under
the covers. D.L. looks into room 11 and sees JOHN and TINA in*

bed. She turns quickly to LAURA.)

D.L. I don't think you should see this.
LAURA. See what?
D.L.. Why don't you wait out on the terrace?
LAURA. But you said we should wait here.
D.L. Just trust me please.
LAURA. *(Pushes past D.L. and sees JOHN and TINA.)* Oh John!

(She rushes out of 13 and exits sobbing to the terrace.)

D.L. *(Watches her go, closes the door of room 13, steps into room 11, closes the connecting door and turns to JOHN.)* Mr. Baker.
JOHN. Yes D.L.
D.L. You must by now be aware of the fact that your first wife did not die of the sleeping sickness in Costa Rica, and is right here in this club.
JOHN. Good heavens!
D.L. Didn't you see her?
JOHN. Well—er—I did but—er—I knew she was dead, so I thought I must be hallucinating.
D.L. *(Sits on the L. edge of the bed.)* Oh you poor dear boy.
JOHN. Yes.
D.L. Well, it's true.
JOHN. Oh!
D.L. Yes, she's alive, so under the circumstances, don't you think you ought to call off the honeymoon?
JOHN. Honeymoon?
D.L. I think perhaps we had better tell your new wife. Is she asleep?

(D.L. leans R. over the bed in order to look at TINA, and puts her L. hand for support right where DAVID'S crotch would be. There is a loud yell from DAVID, followed by a long agonizing groan. D. L. leaps up and looks at the bed. JOHN thumps the hidden figure of DAVID and takes up the groan himself.)

JOHN. A-e-i-o-o-o-gh!

D.L. Are you alright?

JOHN. Just a little indigestion.

TINA. *(The yelling has woken her up.)* I'm ready for a little drink. *(She pours champagne into her glass.)* Let's celebrate.

D.L. Celebrate? Oh my goodness—you haven't?—I mean, it's not too late is it?—I mean—has the honeymoon started?

TINA. That's it, that's what we were going to do.

(She puts down her glass and reaches sexily for JOHN, who gently fends her off.)

D.L. Mr. Baker, may I suggest you get out of bed and get dressed while I go and bring your wife back so we can all discuss this situation like adults.

(Exits room 11, closing the door, then R. on the terrace. Enter MRS. CARLSON from the office. She goes U. then L. on the landing, enters room 13, and listens outside the connecting door.)

JOHN. Now what? She's gone to get Laura.

(TINA slumps down and goes to sleep again.)

DAVID. One step at a time. I need you as my wife, one more time. *(He hands JOHN the wig.)* Hurry, get dressed.

JOHN. *(Goes into the bathroom, picks up the dress from the floor and starts to put it on.) (Off.)* What are we going to do now, we're getting into a worse mess.

DAVID. I'm the one who's in a mess, you're O.K.

JOHN. *(Off.)* What do you mean, I'm O.K. D.L. thinks I've got two wives.

DAVID. Yeah, but it's all perfectly logical. Laura survived the sleeping sickness, but you didn't know and got married again.

JOHN. *(Off.)* Well, we might get away with that as long as Laura agrees to go along with it.

DAVID. I'm sure she will. First chance you get tell her the truth about the other Mrs. Baker and how it all happened.

MRS. C. *(Opens the connecting door and steps into the room.)* Perhaps you should tell us all the truth about the other Mrs. Baker!

DAVID. Well—er—you see the first Mrs. Baker got a disease and died.

MRS. C. Oh, what disease?

DAVID. She was bitten by a tsetse fly.

MRS. C. In Connecticut?

DAVID. They were on vacation in Costa Rica.

MRS. C. Rubbish! I knew that Baker character was a no-good womanizer. I could tell the minute I set eyes on him. I'm surprised at you Mr. McGachen, covering up for him like that.

DAVID. No, no, Mrs. Carlson. I can explain. He doesn't really have two wives.

MRS. C. Really, then who are you talking to in the bathroom and who is this other Mrs. Baker?

DAVID. What other Mrs. Baker?

MRS. C. The one in the bathroom.

DAVID. Ah yes. That Mrs. Baker. *(He pauses, racking his brains.)* That's—er—that's John Baker's mother.

(JOHN, now in wig and dress, and visible to the audience in the doorway of the bathroom, reacts.)

MRS. C. What?

DAVID. John Baker's mother. She'll be out in a minute, won't you Mother Baker?

(JOHN ties a small linen towel over his head like a scarf, and frantically dumps talcum powder on the front of his hair.)

MRS. C. I didn't know his mother was here.

DAVID. Oh yes. He's such a good boy, he doesn't like to leave his mother alone at home. *(JOHN steps into the room.)* Let me introduce you. Mrs. Carlson, this is John's mother.

MRS. C. His mother?

DAVID. Yes, can't you see the family resemblance? Mother

Baker, meet Mrs. Carlson.

JOHN. *(Comes D. to the foot of the bed to shake hands.)* How do you do?

MRS. C. I'm pleased to meet you Mrs. Baker.

JOHN   You've—er—met my son then?

MRS. C. *(Almost to herself.)* I wonder if I might have misjudged him.

JOHN. He's such a dear sweet boy don't you think?

MRS. C. Well, yes I suppose so.

DAVID. And now, much as we enjoy your company Mrs. Carlson, if you'll excuse us, we do have things to do.

MRS. C. Yes, yes, of course. *(She turns to go, then turns back into the room.)* His mother?

DAVID. Of course.

MRS. C. I'm very confused. What's her name?

There is a slight pause as JOHN and DAVID look at each other.)

JOHN. *(Together.)* Annabella
DAVID. *(Together.)* Esmerelda
JOHN. *(Together.)* Esmerelda
DAVID. *(Together.)* Annabella
DAVID. Er—Annabella Esmerelda
MRS. C. *(Incredulous.)* Annabella Esmerelda?
DAVID. Annabella Esmerelda.

DAVID and JOHN smile at MRS. CARLSON, who shakes her head, exits room 11, then comes D. and into the office.)

JOHN. Now what?

DAVID. *(Looks nervously out of the door of room 11, then R. along the hallway.)* Give me a minute...I've got it, get into bed in this room.

He indicates 13.)

JOHN. *(Takes off the towel and dusts off the wig.)* Yes my little pumpkin. Am I me, my sister, your wife or my own mother?

(They go into 13.)

DAVID. You're my wife, one last time so D.L. knows where you are. Now just sit tight while I go and see where everyone is. *(Exits 13 closing the door then R. on the landing. JOHN exits to bathroom 13, leaving the door ajar. Enter KARLY from the front entrance. DAVID sees her and comes D.)* Karly, we have to talk.

KARLY. I've already told you David. I'm not talking to you.

DAVID. Let me explain. You see we accidentally bumped into the new president of Ashley Maureen, who said no-one could work for the new corporation who went golfing without their wives. So we had to produce some wives. It's as simple as that.

KARLY. That's wonderful and very interesting, and whenever you're ready to tell me the truth I'll be listening.

DAVID. Karly, listen to me, there's all sorts of things you don't know.

KARLY. I'm sorry, but I'll be busy all evening.

DAVID. What do you mean, busy?

KARLY. *(Crosses L. and sits in the chair.)* If you must know Laura and I have just made dates for this evening.

DAVID. *(Sits on the sofa.)* You and little Laura? That's ridiculous.

KARLY. What do you mean, me and little Laura, and what's ridiculous about it?

DAVID. In the first place, I know you don't mean it, and in the second place, the club's empty, there's nobody here.

KARLY. There most certainly is. I don't mind telling you that Laura and I have met two very attractive people.

DAVID. Who?

KARLY. I won't embarrass you by telling you the name of my date, you'll find out soon enough anyway, but I'm sure Laura wouldn't mind my telling you that she's going out this evening, on a very romantic date, with D.L. Hutchison.

DAVID. *(Incredulous.)* D.L.?

KARLY. And what's more, I'm going to ask my new boyfriend

to make it a foursome. What do you think of that?

DAVID. Laura and D.L.?

KARLY. Oh yes. Let's see how Mr. Baker likes that.

DAVID. I would never have guessed it. Are you sure?

KARLY. Of course I'm sure. We discussed it together.

DAVID. Things are really getting out of hand. How long has Laura been like that?

KARLY. Like what?

DAVID. Well, you know, romantically interested in other — you know.

KARLY. It was probably seeing you and John fooling around that sent her over the edge.

DAVID. Oh Karly, I've told you, we weren't fooling around. Does John have any idea?

KARLY. Probably not, but he's going to find out real soon.

DAVID. He'll be devastated.

KARLY. You seem more concerned about Laura and D.L. than you do about me and my boyfriend.

DAVID. Well, the idea takes a bit of getting used to. I mean Laura and D.L.?

KARLY. *(Stands and heads U.)* If that's all you can talk about, I'm going up to our room to get ready for my date.

DAVID. *(Follows her.)* Listen, Karly, I know you don't have a boyfriend, please just stay here for a minute. I've got to find D.L., then I'll be right back, please?

(He rushes off R. to the terrace.)

KARLY. I'll show him who's got a boyfriend. *(She comes back D. to the counter and rings the call bell. Enter MRS. CARLSON.)* Ah, Mrs. Carlson. I wonder if perhaps you could send Wilson up to change the phone in room 11. We seem to be having all sorts of problems with it.

MRS. C. Of course, I'll have him there right away.

(Exits to office.)

KARLY. Thank you.

(She hurries U. and goes into room 11. She looks into room 13, sees no one and carefully closes the connecting door, leaving it just an inch or two open. She primps a little as WILSON comes out of the office with a phone in his hand, comes up to room 11 and taps on the open door.)

KARLY. Do come in Wilson.
WILSON. *(Looking at her very suspiciously.)* Mrs. C. said you wanted a new phone.
KARLY. Yes, thank you.
WILSON. It won't do any good, it's the wiring that's on the blink, not the phones.
KARLY. Well, let's at least try shall we?

(WILSON moves carefully past KARLY, side-stepping so as not to get too close to her, and moves to the R. side of the bed. He bends down and fiddles with the wires as D.L. and DAVID enter from the terrace and cross L. to 13. KARLY listens at the connecting door.)

DAVID. I'm sorry D.L. I don't know where John is. *(They enter 13.)* I'm afraid I really can't help you. *(Sees the empty bed.)* Where are you pumpkin?
JOHN. *(Enters from bathroom 13 carrying a small towel.)* Here I am my little peach blossom.

(He gets into bed.)

DAVID. *(Kicks off his shoes and gets into bed with JOHN.)* Are you comfy sweetheart?

(Puts his arm around JOHN. KARLY, listening at the connecting door, reacts by mouthing the words, "pumpkin", "peach blossom" and "sweetheart" to the audience then moves R. around the foot of the bed to WILSON.)

KARLY. Alone together at last.

WILSON. *(Stands up.)* Oh Lord, here we go again.

KARLY. Wilson, let's go out together tonight.

WILSON. What if your husband sees us?

KARLY. That's the idea. Wilson, would you be embarrassed if I kissed you in a public place?

WILSON. Not nearly as much as if you kissed me in a private place.

KARLY. Let's do it. *(As KARLY comes round the foot of the bed, WILSON looks for a way of escape, first at the bathroom, he decides against that, and climbs over the bed. KARLY waits till he is over TINA, about in the middle of the bed, then quickly makes her move to intercept him before he can get to the door. On the run, she opens the connecting door a little more, then turns R. to WILSON.)* I need a real man!

(She flings herself at WILSON on the bed as TINA sits up.)

TINA. *(Very sleepy.)* It's honeymoon time.

(She tries to kiss WILSON and manages to kiss him on his R. cheek. KARLY kisses him on the L. cheek as D.L. opens the connecting door. MRS. CARLSON enters from the office and comes U. then L. on the landing.)

D.L. Wilson? Mrs. Baker? And who are you?

KARLY. I'm Mrs. McGachen.

D.L. You can't be Mrs. McGachen. She's in bed in the other room.

(TINA picks up her glass and is drinking as MRS. CARLSON bursts into room 11. WILSON, quick as a flash ducks under the covers and is not seen by MRS. CARLSON.)

MRS. C. Tina, what do you think you're doing?

TINA. *(Giggles.)* I'm honeying my moon, I mean I'm mooning my honey.

MRS. C. Oh. This is too much. Drinking in one of the guest rooms. Tina, I simply cannot tolerate this. I'm afraid you're fired. *(She glances through the connecting door, pushes D.L. to one side and steps into 13. JOHN has quickly draped the towel over his head like a scarf.)* Mr. McGachen, what are you doing in bed with Mr. Baker's mother?

KARLY. *(Hearing this, gets off the bed and rushes into 13.)* Oh no, they're at it again.

(Everybody talks at once.)

    D.L. Who?
    DAVID. Let me explain.
    D.L. Mr. Baker's mother?
    TINA. Let's all have another drink.
    MRS. C. This to too much.
    KARLY. Darn right its too much.

(Everybody joins in.)

JOHN. STOP. *(Pulls the wig off his head and gets out of bed.)* I've had it. I don't care if we all get fired. I can't take any more o this. D.L., David and I were here for a golfing weekend without ou wives, but only because they wanted to get away shopping. When you said no-one who did that would ever work for you, I became Mrs McGachen and Tina in there, who works here, volunteered to be Mrs Baker. We had no idea our real wives were going to show up, and frankly, you can fire me if you want to, but my marriage is worth more than all this. And now, if you'll excuse me, I am going to find my wife, explain everything to her, and hope she'll forgive me.

(Exits room 13, then R. to the terrace.)

MRS. C. Well perhaps things can get back to normal around here *(She goes back into room 11 and is about to exit when she stops pauses and calls over her shoulder.)* You can get out of that bed Wil son. I want to see you in the office.

(She exits room 11, comes D. and exits to the office. WILSON appears from under the bedclothes, grins at everyone and follows her.)

D.L. *(Goes back into 11, and helps TINA off the bed and into the bathroom.)* If you get dressed my dear, I'll drive you home. *(TINA goes into the bathroom and D.L. stands talking to the open door.)* You know you really are a very enterprising young lady. I'd like you to come and work for the Ashley Maureen Corporation. There are going to be a number of job openings in very senior positions.

KARLY. *(In room 13.)* Oh David, you did all that for me?

(She gets on the bed with him.)

DAVID. Well, we had to do something.

KARLY. Oh David!

(They embrace. The counter phone rings. Enter MRS. CARLSON from the office.)

MRS. C. *(Picks up the phone.)* Oakfield Golf and Country Club. Mrs. Hutchison? Yes she's here. May I tell her who's calling? Oh, Mr. Hutchison, one moment sir, she was in room 11 a minute ago. I'll try to put you through. I hope it works, we've been having problems with the phones all day, but here goes.

(She pushes buttons, the phone rings in room 11. D.L. picks it up.)

D.L. Hello.

MRS. C. Mrs. Hutchison?

D.L. Yes.

MRS. C. Just a moment please, I have Mr. Hutchison on the line.

(She pushes buttons again. MR. HUTCHISON's voice now comes over the loud speakers.)

MR. H. Dorothy?

D.L. Oliver!

MR. H. Who else.

D.L. How did you get my number?

MR. H. Oh I've had your number for a long time.

MRS. C. *(Rushes into the office.)* Wilson!

D.L. Maybe you could call me later dear, your voice appears to be coming over the intercom system.

MR. H. I don't care if my voice is being broadcast over every radio and TV station in New England. I've told you before, I will not have you sneaking off alone to play golf on weekends. It's become an obsession with you and it's got to stop. Now get in your car and get yourself home to your family. Now!

(DAVID and KARLY react.)

D.L. But Oliver—hello—hello—Oh dear he hung up.

TINA. *(Comes out of the bathroom, now dressed.)* He sounded kinda mad.

D.L. Yes he did, didn't he. I'll have to go. I'll take you home first. I don't think you should be driving.

(They exit room 11 and go R. on the landing.)

KARLY. Did you hear that?

DAVID. I sure did. The fat lady really does have laryngitis. We're in the clear.

KARLY. Oh David!

DAVID. Oh Karly!

(They roll over on the bed in a passionate embrace.)

TINA. *(As they come D.)* Do you really mean it, you have a job for me?

D.L. Absolutely, we can definitely use someone like you at Ashley Maureen.

(Exits front entrance. Enter JOHN and LAURA from the terrace arms around each other.)

JOHN. So you see that's how it all happened.
LAURA. I forgive you John.

(They stop at the top of the stairs and give each other a passionate kiss, as WILSON enters from the office. JOHN'S head is U.S. and hidden from him. What he sees are two female figures embracing. He pauses, looks, then turns to the audience and silently mouths the words "I don't believe it". JOHN and LAURA continue on to room 11, close the door, and embrace as they fall together on the bed. The table phone rings. WILSON looks furtively into the office then walks quickly over to the table phone. He takes a cellular phone out of his pocket.)

WILSON. Yeah? *(He takes a small black book and a pencil out of another pocket.)* Yeah, it's me. Sorry about that, the phones have been screwed up around here today. What? Of course I can. Right. *(He writes in the book.)* I've got it. Twenty bucks on Golden Girl. You're in the book. For you Harry. Eight to one. Good luck. *(He pockets the phone and walks over to the office door.)* Goodnight Mrs. C.

(He exits out the front entrance with a hop, skip and a jump.)

MRS. C. *(Puts her head out of the office door.)* Goodnight Wilson.

(She turns out of the lobby lights and exits to the office.)

KARLY. Goodnight David.
LAURA. Goodnight John Boy.
DAVID. *(Turns out the lights in room 13.)* Goodnight my little peach blossom.
JOHN. *(Turns out the lights in room 11.)* Goodnight pumpkin.

(In the darkness the curtain falls.)

End

COSTUME PLOT

JOHN BAKER
>   Sport shirt
>   Tan slacks
>   Socks
>   Dress shoes
>   Female wig
>   Woman's dress
>   Woman's shoes
>   T-shirt
>   Boxers

DAVID McGECHAN
>   Sport shirt
>   Slacks
>   Socks
>   Dress shoes

TINA
>   Fitted skirt
>   Long-sleeved silk blouse
>   Hose
>   High-hell pumps or sandals
>   Suit jacket
>   Full slip
>   Bra
>   Tap pants

MRS. CARLSON
>   Conservative summer suit
>   Blouse
>   Hose
>   Dress shoes

WILSON
    Golf shirt
    Tan pants
    Shoes
    Socks

D.L. HUTCHISON
    Pastel summer suit
    Blouse
    Hose
    High-hell pumps or sandals
    Half slip
    Appropriate underwear

LAURA
    Skirt
    Blouse
    Hose
    Shoes

KARLY
    Summer dress
    Hose
    Shoes

FURNITURE AND PROPERTY LIST

Act I: On Stage

Telephones: Counter
                  Reception area
                  Room 11
                  Room 13
Call bell
Couch
Easy chair
End table
Cushions
Afghan
Newspaper
2 double beds with linens, pillows, bedspreads, etc.
2 bedside tables
2 lamps
Registration forms
Room keys

Act I: Off Stage

Suitcase	(John)
Suitcase	(David)
Golf bag	(John)
Golf bag	(Wilson)
Phone	(Tina)
Purse with bills	(D.L.)
Putter	(David)
Box and shopping bag	(John)
Phone (with cord in office)	(Tina)
Vase and roses	(Wilson)

Bills	(D.L.)
Purse	(Tina)
Tools and wires	(Wilson)
Champagne, ice bucket, 2	
glasses, tray and card	(Wilson)
Two large shopping bags	(Laura)
Two large shopping bags	(Karly)
Small suitcase	(Laura)
Small suitcase	(Karly)

Act II: Off Stage

Phone with lead	(Wilson)
Champagne bottle and glass	(D.L.)
Towel	(D.L.)
Skirt, slip and jacket	(D.L.)
Skirt and slip	(John)
Telephone wires	(Wilson)
Champagne bottle	(Wilson)
Small linen hand towel	(John)
Talcum powder	(John)

Personal

Dollar Bills	(David)
Card	(D.L.)
Dollar Bills	(Laura)
White Handkerchief	(Wilson)
20 bill	(Karly)
Cell phone	(Wilson)
Notebook and pencil	(Wilson)

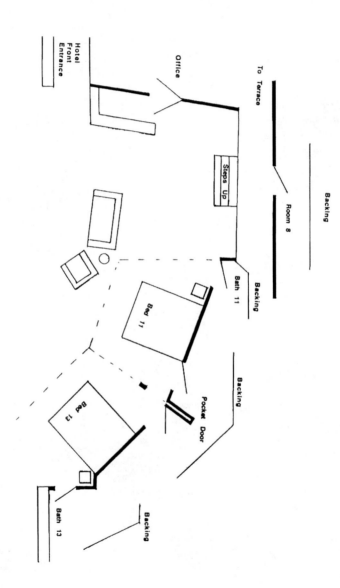

Works by
Michael Parker...

The Amorous Ambassador

Hotbed Hotel

The Lone Star Love Potion

Never Kiss a Naughty Nanny

The Sensuous Senator

There's a Burglar in My Bed

Who's in Bed with the Butler

Whose Wives Are They Anyway?

(with Susan Parker)

Sex Please We're Sixty!

Sin, Sex, and the C.I.A.

What is Susan's Secret?

SIN, SEX & THE C.I.A.

Michael Parker and Susan Parker

Comedy / 3m, 4f

Huge oil reserves have been discovered in The Chagos Islands. O.P.E.C. is pressuring the Chagosians to join the cartel. A C.I.A. agent and an under secretary of State, whose life appears to be run by her libido, are sent to a C.I.A. safe house in the mountains of Virginia to begin negotiations for the U.S. to place the Chagos Islands under their protection. Unfortunately, no one knows who the islands' representative really is. We are left to wonder how the C.I.A. agent ever got the job. He gets caught in all his own booby traps, he electrocutes himself, he sets fire to himself, he gets a bucket stuck on his head, and finally locks himself in his own handcuffs! Add to the inevitable chaos, a stranded televangelist, his innocent secretary (or is she?), an ex-marine caretaker, who isn't what he seems to be, and a mysterious, glamorous neighbor, and you have a complex, laugh out loud farce, that can be played on any stage.

"This play has character development, as every good play must."
"The plot has more turns than Soda Bay Road."
– *Record Bee,* Lakeport, California

"*Sin, Sex & the C.I.A.* generously incorporates every aspect of farcical comedy into its insanely funny script."
– Hemet, California

"Packed with double entendres and lot of humor"
"….comic moments and hearty laughs."
– *Sarasota Herald Tribune,* Sarasota, Florida

"Nearly every element of comic farce is present in this show – for an audience that means laughter from beginning to end!"
– Paradise Playhouse, Excelsior Springs, MO

"Laugh out loud hilarity…the laughs are relentless."
– *The Press-enterprise,* California

"Rib splittingly funny"
"A complex and hilariously funny plot"
"The Parkers are masters at this style of theatre"
– *Englewood Sun Herald,* Englewood, Florida

OTHER TITLES AVAILABLE FROM SAMUEL FRENCH

NEVER KISS A NAUGHTY NANNY

Michael Parker

Farce / 4 or 5m, 3f / Interior

Mr. Broadbent, a developer and builder, has created "THE HOUSE OF THE FUTURE". He has filled it with gadgets such as: self lighting fire places, a self cleaning bathroom, central trash disposal units, automatic closets, hidden telephones, and his masterpiece "The Personal Ion Chamber." The house, however, has remained unsold for four years, probably because, as we see in the course of the play, most of the innovations of the future fail to work properly.

He has, at last, found prospective buyers, Fred and Gladys McNicoll, and invites them to stay in the house. He is determined to offload this huge "White Elephant." He bribes two members of his staff, Casey Cody and Ben Adams, to pose as a married couple, who are renting the house. They are to extol its virtues and explain how everything works. He is pulling out all the stops. The fridge is full of expensive wine and he has hired a chef to prepare a gourmet meal. Unknown to The McNicolls', he even has his maintenance man Eddie Cott on hand to make running repairs. He thinks he has all the bases covered.

When Gladys hears Casey refer to Mr. Cott by name, the cat seems to be out of the bag, but Casey quickly recovers by saying she didn't say "Mister Cott" but "Ms. Turcotte", the children's nanny. Eddie Cott now spends the rest of the play as Nanny Turcotte. A surprise visitor, Mr. Brooks, takes an almost insane fancy to "Nanny" who now has to defend 'her' honor, as well as fix the gadgets, all of which, without exception, misbehave.

> "In this play, technology that doesn't work is just plain fun. Two hours of enjoyment and laughter." – *The Seminole Beacon*, Tampa

> "I was laughing so much I could barely hold the camera still."
> – WVTV Fox 13, Tampa - St. Petersberg

> "Its many twists and turns make *Never Kiss a Naughty Nanny* a classic farce, which is sure to bring a smile." – *The Citizen*, Clearwater

OTHER TITLES AVAILABLE FROM SAMUEL FRENCH

SEX PLEASE, WE'RE SIXTY!

Michael Parker and Susan Parker

Farce / 2m, 4f

Mrs. Stancliffe's Rose Cottage Bed & Breakfast has been successful for many years. Her guests (nearly all women) return year after year. Her next door neighbor, the elderly, silver-tongued, Bud "Bud the Stud" Davis believes they come to spend time with him in romantic liaisons. The prim and proper Mrs. Stancliffe steadfastly denies this, but really doesn't do anything to prevent it. She reluctantly accepts the fact that "Bud the Stud" is, in fact, good for business. Her other neighbor and would-be suitor Henry Mitchell is a retired chemist who has developed a blue pill called "Venusia," after Venus the goddess of love, to increase the libido of menopausal women. The pill has not been tested. Add to the guest list three older women: Victoria Ambrose, a romance novelist whose personal life seems to be lacking in romance; Hillary Hudson, a friend of Henry's who has agreed to test the Venusia: and Charmaine Beauregard, a "Southern Belle" whose libido does not need to be increased! Bud gets his hands on some of the Venusia pills and the fun begins, as he attempts to entertain all three women! The women mix up Bud's Viagra pills with the Venusia, and we soon discover that it has a strange effect on men: it gives them all the symptoms of menopausal women, complete with hot flashes, mood swings, weeping and irritability! When the mayhem settles down, all the women find their lives moving in new and surprising directions.

"This play is a winner."
- Rocky Varcoe. Owner & CEO Class Act Dinner Theatre, Toronto, Canada

"Fast paced and hilarious."
- *The Californian*